The Dread Road

by Meridel Le Sueur

The Dread Road

by Meridel Le Sueur

with editorial assistance from
Rachel Tilsen, John Crawford,
Michael Reed *and* Patricia Clark Smith

West End Press

1991

A portion of the core narrative of this story, from an earlier manuscript version, appeared in *Hurricane Alice: a feminist quarterly*, vol. 5, no. 3, summer 1988, 1–3.

Cover photographs of details of the statue at Ludlow memorial and of Meridel Le Sueur at Ludlow memorial were taken by Deborah Le Sueur in 1985 and are used with her permission. All rights reserved.

The three inside illustrations, inspired by this story, are by Rosa De Anda and used with her permission. All rights reserved.

This work is partially supported by a grant from the National Endowment for the Arts, a federal agency.

Made in the United States of America.
First printing 1991.

Typography, design, and production by Michael Reed of Prototype, Albuquerque, New Mexico.

ISBN 0-931122-63-5
$11.95

West End Press   •   P.O. Box 27334   •   Albuquerque, NM 87125

For the women on the Dread Road of this earth,
carrying the starved and poisoned children.

During the whole of a dull, dark, and soundless day in the autumn of the year, when the clouds hung oppressively low in the heavens, I had been passing alone, on horseback, through a singularly dreary tract of country, and at length found myself, as the shades of the evening drew on, within view of the melancholy house of Usher. I know not how it was—but, with the first glimpse of the building, a sense of insufferable gloom pervaded my spirit.[1]

Here again I paused abruptly, and now with a feeling of wild amazement—for there could be no doubt whatever, that in this distance, I did actually hear (although from what direction it proceeded I found it impossible to say) a low and apparently distant, but harsh, protracted, and most unusual screaming or grating sound. . . .[2]

As always in November I took the dread road north from Albuquerque, through the injured haunted earth to see my son, buried but not dead in Denver, where the mutants are, the distorted, the children who it is said were born with the poison of nuclear fallout from the Nevada bomb test or the nuclear waste now coming in from Missouri . . . children with no faces, no arms, with strange inner viruses and brain damage.

I hid him there after he was born, too early, not early enough to be dead. I was a young pregnant wife when they made that test, killed the sheep and the fish and the foliage . . . changed the genes, the seed, forever. I hid his awful condition there and went to see him twice a year, and he didn't know me.

I used to take tranquilizers going the dread road north through the injured earth, through the oblique horizontal valley of the massacres, the mining hills where our fathers slaved in the dark for hardly enough to feed their children . . . filled with ghosts, veering the bus in sorcerers' winds.

I took the pills before we got to Trinidad, toward Ludlow flying, penetrating the distance . . . where Louis Tikas was riddled with 85 bullets fired point-blank as he tried to protect the children underground in the cave below the tent. You can lift a cellarlike door now by the monument and you can descend into that pit and hear the cries of the children.

I would wait for the night to take that terrible journey along this dread road, trying not to remember my grandparents killed in the mine strike in Ludlow, to

I have come on this road how many years, the road of my husband, poisoned from the fallout, and now my mutilated child, his mouth awry, his blind eye on his cheek. We were assured by the government the fallout was harmless. I stood in court and said it. I came on this lying road, on their accusing corpses. This is the dread road toward the corpse, the hidden dead. I have been part of the conspiracy through the deep shifting mist, the crying of the corpses.

The earth is a history of wind, time, men and women, every kind of hoof, foot, cloven and Christian . . . the earth forgets rejects insults nobody . . . great folk lay down, pachyderm alight, twitching below the hills. The hills run like red burning mares beside you . . . loping as if in heat . . . toward stallions . . . hair flying, pursuing the stallion sun . . . shaking his fiery mane, thrusting his great golden tongue into all crevasses. . . .

Blood spills on the plowed earth, the crows scream overhead. Worms unite and form black wings, underground rocks are stained with blood.

I beseech you we are part of you part of each other.

1

close my eyes as we went through in the dark so you could not even see the United Mine Workers sign pointing to their statue in commemoration of those who died there, with the woman and the man over the dead children pointing to the hole where they were killed.

The bus came in from El Paso, picking up Mexican passengers, some undocumented workers too, along the way. The police went through the bus at regular intervals, armed to the teeth.

There were not many in the Albuquerque station as I got my round-trip ticket. Several old men were sleeping and then I saw her sitting bold upright under the high arches near the ladies' room. It was like coming suddenly upon a terrible accident that had just happened. Startling, a fire, something broken and burning.

There was no logic to the effect it had on me. I felt struck in my flesh, in my heart, in my womb.

She was a dark young woman in jeans and an old coat and an imitation leather hat tight on black straight hair that seemed to move around her dead-white face, and on her lap crosswise she held tightly to a zipper bag you buy at the drug store for six or seven dollars. It zips open on three sides, and this one had bright red roses printed all over it, and she held onto it with hands that were red and bloodied. She sat straight up, burning like a fire in a heinous accident.

Others felt it too. An old Indian couple saw her and veered away and sat across from her, and at the same time a large white big-boned woman bore toward me and, with the same startled feeling I had, said in a low voice, "Who is she?"

There were many individuals in the crowd who had found leisure to become aware of the presence of a masked figure which had arrested the attention of no single individual before. And the rumor of this new presence having spread itself whisperingly around, there arose at length from the whole company a buzz, or murmur, expressive of disapprobation and surprise—then, finally, of terror, of horror, and of disgust.[3]

Look in the windows. I always looked in the windows in America . . . floundering rotten boats, rusted men. Open your hand and gather the clustered light of space. Open your mouth and the black fruit night grape falls in bursts on your tongue. The owl with its great striped wings flies into your tree and sits all day in your arm branches . . . flies before you hovering over you its wings outspread.

I demand that you listen. Be with me on the dread journey, that dread road we must take now. We must all take this journey into each other, into the dark but luminous heart, into the human power of memory and time in the menaced arteries, radiation striking, mutilation, we can be skinned alive without knowing it or saying a word. Luminous and secret I summon our memory, the loving memory that is our transformation.

We only recognize it when it is sudden and the blood spurts on us. We do not see the journey coming down the road.

Court opens, millions appear . . . come to judgment.

"I don't know," I said, irritated. "I don't know who she is."

"She's in trouble," the big woman said with a conspiratorial and accusing air which made me angry.

She was a tall thin woman who brought order with her. She saw the girl with the zipper bag and stood still a moment, looking at her like a bird dog flushing her out. The girl gripped the bag tighter and I saw her with the eyes of this woman for a moment. First it appeared she was going to sit next to her. You saw her direction, her orderly decisions, and a frightening kind of implacable energy. Instead, she deliberately crossed the aisle and sat beside me so we both were opposite the burning girl.

"She's probably frightened," I said.

Just then a gang of young skiers going to the Colorado mountains came through the door with all their paraphernalia and three sheets to the wind, hilarious.

At the same time that they were loading all their ski equipment in the opposite aisle, I saw the bus driver behind the ticket window looking into the station. I saw the skiers hesitate as they saw her burning. Their loud talk lowered when they all saw her.

One of them taking his big pack off said to her, "You going to Denver?"

She said in a muffled voice, "I didn't have to go by bus . . . I came down. I flew down."

"Wow," he said, "the bus is OK, though, you can sleep if you have a little hot juice in you."

We were no longer on a little journey. . . . She made our present strangely break open, as a sudden collision of a summer day breaks open the squares and boxes, throws the bodies into terrible postures of decay and death, ripped in body, gashed in spirit . . . a terrible sense closed in in that tiny metal square of something pending, something about to destroy us, something with terrible intent, our fathers crawling underground, entombed, buried without bell or candle. Even the earth gutted, slashed, thrown up, turned inside out, its mother fertility violated. Insufferable gloom of our terrible accident, greed and power, terrible and violent. We were traveling through a wound.

They believe we are enemies. They speak nothing about the enemy, the dangers, the killing, they don't say a word. Fine thread sews their eyes shut, thread of gold sews their nightingale tongues shut, stitches their mouths shut. They do not endanger the conqueror.

This is my fire. This is my body. This is my shadow. These are my dead. Stay out of me. Stay out of my blood. Stay out of my work. I've got a strong life you do not know.

"Hey, kid," another said, "want me to put your bag down? No use holding it like that. We'll help you on the bus."

"No. No," she cried out and held the bag upward on her breast.

"OK, baby, no harm meant. Take it cool . . . take it cool."

The bus driver was coming toward her. I could see why. She seemed to spring into you as if you no longer saw an object outside you but she sprang into you, as I say, like a terrible thing happening . . . a conflagration.

The young skiers, great rowdy boys, had gotten their tickets and now poured around us, joshing and kidding, but they turned up frightened eyes, feeling something strange coming. "She's got something in the bag," one said. "Maybe a bomb . . . maybe she come over the border with some dope. Come on baby, give . . . it's getting harder to get. She's in the gravy, no kiddin'."

Then to my horror came two station cops armed to the gills, two pistols, billy clubs, one long gun, walkie-talkies. "You got your ticket, miss? No pickups here." They were huge men leaning down over her.

In a kind of terror like someone who had just been in a terrible crash, a shock, she found her ticket, looking first in her coat pocket and then finding it in her jeans pocket, still holding to the flowered bag like a raft as if she was sinking without it.

The white woman got up and stood behind them. What was she going to do? The cops backing away from the burning girl bumped into the woman, who

Despite all we went unarmed. Persephone dancing toward the asphodel.

Refined words covering the violence. Keep talking and you won't hear.

It is a wild thing in women, a constructive wildness not recognized. Men make a whore of it and demand virtuous women. . . . Only the seed knows what to do with the power of life. Compulsion of the root expressed in the seed.

My lost, hush, my sister, my lone my lonely one, crying from the high willow, tit willow. Who marries on the road to Katoa on a pollen gold day. Sing your way to beds of hay, crawl into hay ricks, the dugs of goats and cows, sing if you can, apple be ripe and pears be brown, petticoats up and trousers down, old wanderers sliced from stem to stern by the stove poker. Ancient angel prairie seer punksuckler blue.

Blinded by ghostly images, women see themselves as immensely productive potential. Bring forth value out of being together. Space, prairie emptiness to be filled, calling for human fulfillment.

I was sick—sick unto death with long agony; and when they at length unbound me, and I was permitted to sit, I felt that my senses were leaving me. . . . I saw the lips of the black-robed judges. They appeared to me white, whiter than the sheet upon which I trace these words, and thin even to grotesqueness; thin with the intensity of their expression of firmness—of immovable resolution, of stern contempt of human torture.[4]

drew them away and like some hound dog began to pant and say something about the girl. I didn't know what it was but the cops finally shook their heads, looked at the girl and walked away.

The woman was going toward the girl, who rose clutching the bag, still holding it crosswise in her arms. The woman, like a terrible inquisitor, followed her. She was going to the rest room.

The station was filling now with passengers and I watched each one sense something wrong, or the smell of something beyond the mirror of that moment, an apparition beyond that time and place. They came from the ticket window as she was coming back from the rest room, and the big woman was following her like a bloodhound about to tree the victim.

The young woman sat down almost where she had been, as if the rowdy skiers gave her some protection, and the big woman came as if in secret and sat beside me. I had moved across the aisle so I could see her. "She's going to Denver," she said. "She won't talk. There's some funny smell about her. I can always smell trouble."

She leaned over, lowering her head and still looking at the girl. "Have you been here long?" she asked me.

"No," I said.

"We have ten minutes," she said.

"Yes," I said, and saw the driver sorting his tabs and about to open the doors to the Denver bus. "The driver is about ready," I said. I saw that I didn't know him.

She drew back and watched the girl who now was looking straight ahead and her face was pale as if stained white but still flushed.

We have nourished within us the two opposing forces which produce life, now we must choose. Now we must choose not only our behavior . . . which side we are on . . . but we must choose our inmost sense of responsibility. There is a choice of the road to humanity. . . .

America is the biggest graveyard, immense grave, red grave of Indians. Take the starch out of you. Everybody is dead. Rot, stench, a dying, a disaster. Are we dwellers in a dead land, rotting in a sea of howling blood, our great dreaming trampled in massacre? We have a strong case against each other.

"She looks funny to me," the woman said. She wore a strange hat and she took off some short white gloves. Her hands were huge, bony, and efficient. They could grab you.

"Why?" I asked.

"Well, she has a funny color. Very dangerous color."

She did. Her face was like an exaggerated response to nothing that was then visible.

"She looks like a junkie to me," the woman said. Her mouth was invisible, pulled in a straight line, cruel as if she ate strange things.

"Oh, I don't know," I said, leaning to her, fearful the girl might hear me. "She looks like a stoop laborer. Maybe she's between jobs going north to the beets or potatoes."

"She's sick." The woman said it as if she was glad. "Maybe I should speak to her."

"Well, she looks like she needs help," I said. "Maybe she should . . ."

"She has the color of a cocaine addict," she said.

"Oh, I wouldn't jump to conclusions," I said.

"Well, it is dangerous," she said. "Very dangerous. It's my duty to help her."

"Well, let her ask for it. She's not doing anything dangerous," I said. "She seems sad too."

"Well," the woman said, sitting bolt upright now with her strange hat.

The girl seemed to make everything important, suddenly larger, as if something was going to happen.

"Light muffled voice" is the voice of Poe's women after they have been cemented alive in the castle walls. The way her body looked, fortressed, her terrible hips unable to move . . . the sex cemented and hidden.

The Indian woman in prison talked as if under water, she didn't know she was an Indian. She didn't know she was used or what she could have. She spoke inside her hair. It fell over her, she couldn't remember, she had been given shock treatments when she was thirteen. She couldn't remember. She shot a man she didn't even know, couldn't remember his face . . . nothing. She was there for life for what she never knew or never could remember.

[The] story is an apple a squash a bean tomato. It's a direction at the fork of the road, save you from the dangers, lighten the dangers, get you both and the whole nation and the cosmos through . . . into the fruit. We are going to the fruit.

The bus driver, about to announce the departure of the bus, chewing the last of his sandwich and putting on his driver's cap, stood and looked at his passengers. Stood stock still and looked at her. Then he went to the skiers and asked them where they wanted to get off. They joshed with him, "Gonna chase them rabbits like you done before? Sing 'Amazing Grace' like you done? That was fine, and give secret signals to the big cats we pass." The driver smiled and went to ready his bus. And the announcer sang out, "All aboard for Santa Fe, Trinidad, Walsenburg, Pueblo, Denver. No smoking except in the rear of the bus and thanks for going Greyhound."

We all rose and gathered together to line up at the door, and the white woman waited behind her watching her, and one of the boys said kindly to her, "Let me carry your bag, miss, you look plumb tuckered out."

"No. No," she cried, rising and holding it to her body. She was shorter than you might have thought, and she held the flowered bag straight before her like an animal or a child, her arms around it, although the bag had a handle.

The boy looked at her strangely and lined up with his gear and the bus driver took her ticket and she said to him, "I want to get off before we come to the station in Denver."

"I can't do that, we only stop at the station. Do you want to check your bag?"

Purge anything of all its heat . . . as it cools to absolute zero it loses conductivity . . . absence of temperature. The point is you reach a certain stage of temperature and everything is different, all changes, gamut of phase . . . wholes more than parts . . . several metals, alloys, combinations not implied by properties they exhibit in isolation.

Many of us have chosen the road of violence, the road of pessimism, destruction, indifference. Some of us contribute in good faith to making the air unbreathable, a dangerous conductor of destruction, atomic poisons, and pollute the space of those of a different color or place and even of their own children and those children still to be born. Are we to leave a trace of beast upon the earth?

Each woman has a brother to look after, wash all his clothes, take care of him. Who keeps the white clothes of the men clean. Who stays with the children when the man is taken to the U.S. for bloodletting of his labor. At the core of humanity like earth is woman, and the seed is perpetually expanding in time and space.

"No. No," she said, and without shifting the bag she had a hard time getting up the steps and the white woman came right behind her as if driving her in some direction. Inside, the white woman took a second seat.

The bus driver said, "I'll put your bag in the rack." She did not answer but turned from him, and he said, "Sit down there," and she did and I sat next to her, and she was still holding the bag which she carefully turned over a certain way and held there.

"I didn't have to come on the bus. I could've flied," she said. "Nobody can make me. I think that woman behind us is following me. You know her?"

"No," I said, "she's probably a social worker."

A terrible silent fear came over her face and she bent over the bag in an awful protection.

Then I smelled her.

I could feel the white woman behind me, her head above the seat back, vigilant and mean and ghostlike. I could see us all in the darkening glass of the window.

The driver was whistling "Amazing Grace" and making the sign of the cross over the abyss of dark. He flashed off his headlights when a bus or truck passed and they would turn and flash their lights as a signal to the dangerous night ahead, the winter solstice nearing now, the short day, cold over the high pass, truck drivers knowing the hazards, prophets of violent nights, a blessing and a warning to all who traveled this dread road toward Trinidad.

"My," the white woman said, "do you smell something," she said, "like acid?"

He is wondering. He is baffled. Something has happened and he doesn't know what it is. He will be glad when we are gone.

What direction is there. There is no direction. Everything is whirling. Absolute disappearance of spatial directions. We are going toward Denver when it wasn't there or will not be there again.

Yes, Poe said, my fancy grows charnel in the image of gloom. There is the faint phosphorous image now of decay.

The thrust north seizing, entering, the sword of the fathers, Coronado thrusting, then Kansas . . . clear into the golden harvest . . . the armor, the iron met . . . took the food and blankets . . . led them astray in Kansas . . . the mercantile of Spain . . . the making of the maidens . . . seizure back to Spain . . . poor cattle . . . feed the land blood . . . Geronimo . . . the village festival . . . the miners killed them . . . shot upon eating and dancing . . . the oil drills . . . Four Corners . . . open pit . . . Indians dying at Laguna . . . on the lip of the black hole at Ludlow . . . into the mines . . . the children . . . the earth is torn . . . they are not allowed . . . trespassing . . . we own this beach . . . who are they coming from the sea from your sugar cane fields in Haiti.

"Well, they clean the bus in Albuquerque with a disinfectant. That's what it is."

"Oh, yes," she said, leaning her white face forward to look full on us, and her eye traveled to the flowered zipper bag the girl held tightly on her lap, her head lowered over it now. She had taken off her imitation leather hat and she had straight black hair like an Indian. It fell down stiff as black grass. I looked straight ahead but I began to feel her strongly and I saw one foot below me, the toe of the sneakers broken. Then I felt what she was doing. She had a green washrag and she shook her hair back and wiped her face hard, as if to wipe off some terrible web over it. Then she lit a cigarette, and I saw the pallor of her face that was chemical under her brown skin, a ritual color of death. A fright of blood.

The driver swerved the bus sharply and there was a strange sound, a hard bump and sickening thud, and he righted the bus and made a mark on his ticket envelope.

"How many was that?" asked one of the skiers out of the dark. "Nice going, driver. You could knock off a whole generation of rabbits."

"You have to aim accurate. Oh boy, they're quick," he said, "they love the light and then you knock 'em off. If I could stop I could have enough rabbit fur to make a baby bunting to wrap my baby in."

She seemed to have fallen into a sleep, still clutching the bag. Her black hair fell over her face, but she heard him and she said without moving, "You got a baby, driver?" But he didn't hear her.

It was this unfathomable longing of the soul *to vex itself*—to offer violence to its own nature—to do wrong for the wrong's sake only—that urged me to continue and finally to consummate the injury I had inflicted upon the unoffending brute. One morning, in cold blood, I slipped a noose about its neck and hung it to the limb of a tree;—hung it with the tears streaming from my eyes, and with the bitterest remorse at my heart;—hung it *because* I knew it had loved me, and *because* I felt it had given me no reason of offence. . . .[5]

The earth rolls in agony unable to sop up the blood. Bones pulverized on the dread road.

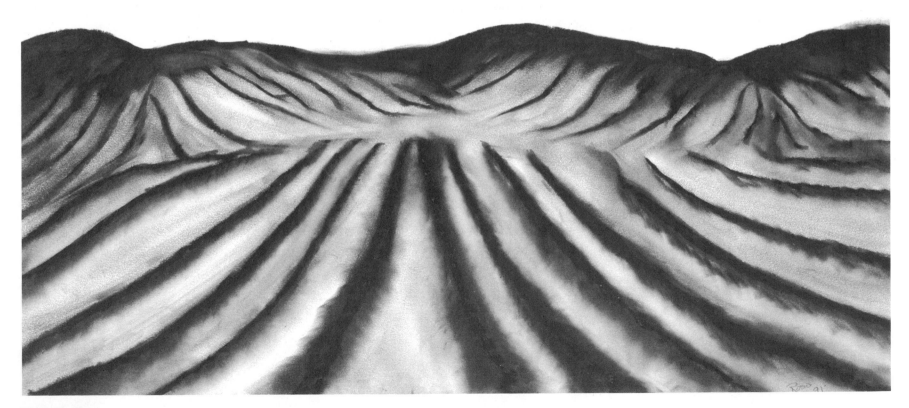

Rosa De Anda

The traffic nearing Santa Fe thinned out and everyone fell into silence and the bus went totally dark when he turned off the lights and flicked them on and off for the great cats going south.

I could see her face in the glass of the window. Her head hung from her curved back over the clutched bag bent to her body. I could smell punk burning, as if something rhythmical lighted up in her, pulsing, distorted, shadowed by some bitter smoking fire.

Seeming asleep, she leaned forward to the bus driver and said, "Don't kill the flies." He said, "Honey, it's bigger game. It's rabbits. Hear that?"

That week a woman had been seized in a parking lot by two men who had not only raped her but cut and broke her skin and opened her with a whiskey bottle. They had put her in the trunk of the car and stopped at taverns in their Saturday night route and shown her for a shot of whiskey, and everyone had come out, men and women, and they had looked and nobody spoke and nobody reported it, and she had died in that pummeling and neglect and insult and nobody had remembered it or reported it or borne witness in any way. One day it was reported, a cursory investigation.

Something was happening, some disaster, all over the earth. Somehow what I felt about my son entered me in a terrible rush and vividness. I was afraid. I was more afraid as we descended over the pass to see the familiar and jagged ruins befouled, broken slag heaps and immense empty mines, earth slums of a century of theft by Rockefeller and Phelps Dodge. Entering Trinidad,

Live in the poisonous gangrenous wound . . . imprisoned in past society inured in nature a compost heap with all its potentials. . . . Apocalypse, no inner and outer. Body and spirit assume one another's attributes . . . forms of what is called real dissolve.

Kali, come to death on the plains of Ludlow. Massacre. Spherical hour. Mother of nomads, seed space. Drop of fire on rail and delicate inhabitants. Gravid, void, ageless, speechless, promiscuous carbonized light, calyx of burning lions in a circle of flames, bread, grail, embers.

You do not scream when you see it between your legs. You are stunned. Everything in you contracts, pulls together, tries to be invisible. It is something rotten inside the nut, something that bears, without mask now comes naked and fearful out of the polluted uterus . . . the poison has entered you. In you, gnawing the fruit, monsters are dreaming, monsters have been conceived by force.

And now the first positive effort to think. And now the first endeavor to remember. And now a partial and evanescent success. And now the memory has so far regained its dominion that, in some measure, I am cognizant of my state. I feel that I am not awaking from ordinary sleep. I recollect that I have been subject to catalepsy.[6]

Unreal!—Even while I breathed there came to my nostrils the breath of the vapor of heated iron! A suffocating odor pervaded the prison. A deeper glow settled each moment in the eyes that glared at my agonies! A richer tint of crimson diffused itself over the pictured horrors of blood.[7]

I looked; and the unseen figure, which still grasped me by the wrist, had caused to be thrown open the graves of all mankind; and from each issued the faint phosphoric radiance of decay; so that I could see into the innermost recesses, and there view the shrouded bodies in their sad and solemn slumbers with the worm. But, alas! the real sleepers were fewer, by many millions, than those who slumbered not at all; and there was a feeble struggling; and there was a general sad unrest; and from out of the depths of the countless pits there came a melancholy rustling from the garments of the buried.[8]

all the old history of the massacre of Ludlow seemed to rise in me like a lost and bright picture.

Why did I go on this terrible journey on this dread road to see my damaged son, hidden, mute, with the terrible eyes out of his mutilated flesh asking me, hidden, unburied, unseen, unwitnessed?

We went over the pass and the open womb of the earth was turned out, hanging out, slag that would last a thousand years like the nuclear atomic terror . . . I dreaded to see the old hotel and the streets empty where they had been full of thousands marching, with the body of Tikas to bury, shot as he tried to protect the tent cellar where the women and children had dug in.

I remember his picture, his Greek face, his tall body and the story my mother used to tell, how Mother Jones came to the funeral, the state militia watching for her . . . she came on the train down from Denver . . . rode with the engineer who let her out before Trinidad and the comrades took her and she rose at the graveside.

I would take the valium now, before we got to the old Trinidad Hotel where the strike committee met and where they brought Tikas with 85 bullets in his strong Greek body. I didn't want to remember how thousands followed his body to the cemetery and Mother Jones spoke, saying "Never forget" as they struck her down, that tender woman.

But somehow I didn't take the valium, somehow I didn't want to sleep. About to enter anew, I was afraid not to, and the waves of nausea and terror deeply hidden came up. "Trinidad," the driver said. "Ten minutes. Remember, ten minutes." The skiers groaned, one wild in some nightmare sleep, and stumbled out for Cokes.

—My son has only one eye and can't tell what he's looking at. And it's down on his cheek.

Never the sun passed over the valley of massacre.

One voice, common song. All the poor break . . . sky swollen like bandages around deserted houses . . . children tried to follow me. Something may stir, cellars without stairs, women cellar exposes naked . . . sudden spaces of tombs deaths voices wind spiders birds and corpses . . . visions obstruct you . . . press against you man with an axe comes toward you to hew the woman tree down.

I want you to listen. We haven't been listening. We haven't been entering each other. Or going through the true country.

There was the same old hotel on the corner in the old mining town of Trinidad. After the terrible massacre of women and children, the runners had run to this hotel to tell the union. It became the center of a world horror. Kansas farmers with their squirrel guns arrived to defend the workers. My grandmother was dead in the black hold, fired upon by Rockefeller goons. And later I had tried to forget it. I had gone to college. I had buried it deep. And now a kind of horror came into me. I thought I couldn't live if I remembered.

I thought, Is this related to the nuclear tests in Nevada? Is it the same thing? A continuation fed by silence? Are we all going to die silent, speechless, mute? I seemed to be near some terrible revelation, the appearance of the enemy who was always killing us, when there was a tap on my shoulder.

Risen, the white woman seemed enormous. In fact, she had to lean her head down from the bus ceiling. She said, "Wouldn't it be good for her to take a little walk? I'll take her for a little walk and a drink." She seemed exhausted.

"No. No," the girl cried. "No. Leave me alone. Leave me alone."

She wouldn't get out. She seemed part of the phosphorous light of the decay. I felt she was glorious in this chemical light, the light from her seemed to contain all history, generative memory, something lost, now remembered. I had let it die.

I followed the woman out of the bus. "Where is she going? What is she going to do? There is something wrong with her," she said.

My mother is running across the plains, coming on the dawn light road. Perhaps she has news. I saw her knocking on the window in the dark. She saw us. She never lost sight of us.

I recognized that in opposite parts of the world, it was the same. With the same enemy. It was the Rockefellers in Ludlow, Phelps Dodge and Anaconda Copper. I see they have their hands in the same body. It was British tea that made slaves, and cinnamon and gold lust and sisal and rubber. They hankered after our wealth, the body of us all. And those few white lepers stole us . . . crept into our beds, into the womb of the earth.

Out of the barren arises the fertile woman remembering everything.

"How do you know? Maybe someone is meeting her?"

"There's something screwy, something wrong. I think she's on something. I've had a lot of experience with these girls."

"Don't do anything, you might be wrong. She's quiet, she isn't hurting anyone or making any trouble. Let her be."

"Well, I'll wait till Pueblo."

I literally ran from her, got in line for a can of Seven-Up and hurried back to the bus.

I didn't want to open the door, pass the sleeping skiers, their huge bodies, innocent, sprawled, seeking pleasure in the wound. Their hideous ignorance and lapse of memory embittered the air, unloosed in the night, illumined by the phosphorous of this incredible girl, the power of poison, the eruption from the putrid air of our memory.

The girl was sitting now, rigid, her eyes wide, fixed, the strange odor of sulphur very strong.

"Here," I said, "take a drink. Have a drink."

She took it eagerly and drank it down and handed me the can.

The last big sleepy skiers returned, carrying bottles like babies to suck on. She half rose and stopped one, then sank back. "I thought that was him. I don't see any of my friends here. They may be coming down to get me. Would you wet this for me?" she said, holding out a green rag.

I had to squeeze by the big woman who was standing in the aisle trying to hear what the girl was saying.

"Sure," I said.

The white woman wants to report something. At least she knows something has been committed. What, she does not know. Maybe it is her own death. Nothing in the world can startle her. She has been chained and electrified, electric shock to take away her memory, soothe her. Upon her brow the sulphuric brand of chemical war.

My child, our child. I saw my crippled child curled as I saw him, his feet never grown, his hand curled, broken buds, the seed nuclear, the seed . . . the sheep died that year. They said the testing was harmless.

To my shame I had my child. The secret psychic landscape has entered me like the radiated air, radiated calcium, it glows in me. The landscape expands day and night in the mushroom blast and that terrible light. It entered my unborn child and convulsed him in terror. His eye went to the wrong place, his cells turned white, his marrow screamed. I see them broken at a distance.

I walked on for several hours, during which the mist deepened around me to so great an extent that at length I was reduced to an absolute groping of the way. And now an indescribable uneasiness possessed me—a species of nervous hesitation and tremor.—I feared to tread, lest I should be precipitated into some abyss. I remembered, too, strange stories told about these Ragged Hills, and of the uncouth and fierce races of men who tenanted their groves and caverns. A thousand vague fancies oppressed and disconcerted me—fancies the more distressing because vague. Very suddenly my attention was arrested by the loud beating of a drum.[9]

When I came back, she took the wet rag and began to claw her face and her wrists, and put the end of the rag in her mouth.

"She's got a fever," the big woman said.

"No," the girl said, "it ain't a fever . . . mind your own business."

"Would you like an aspirin?"

"No," she said. "I got aspirin."

"We're leaving Trinidad," I said, seeing the bare torn womb of the earth scabbed with slag after all these years, wrung inside out.

"Bloody Colorado," she said, "bloody, bloody."

"Yes," I said . . . was she bleeding?

It smelled like blood.

"She'll sleep now," I said. "Let's all sleep. Let's all sleep," I said, "as we pass Ludlow."

"Ludlow," she said.

"It's the queerest thing," the driver said. "There's a piece of road there at night that's out of this world."

"Why?" the woman asked.

"Well, you can't account for it. Strange ghosts seem to be on the road, and terrible winds. Why, a bus was blown clean over on this road. A big bus. I'm telling the truth. I always dread to go through here, I tell you. If you put any store to history, there was a terrible thing happened here before the First World War."

"Ludlow," I said. "The massacre of Ludlow."

"Hang on to your seats, we're entering the big black winds."

History laid over time . . . I saw them gathering. Remembered in the air, written on the night . . . the dark

The valley moves from poisoned vapor, covered up mute broken amputated, to vistas of space and light, informing lighting the heart . . . luminous with conduits of remembering, new vistas of communal time and space opened by another, opened by many old deaths, enter new wombs . . . fluid power of communal memory . . . alive with all in luminosity, transfer of collective memory mounting to immense nuclear light . . . the light from the global flesh, the global human memory.

The earth is not sleeping, she is violated and furious.

They are leaving a message. It is written in the night in the exploding air. Terror of the edge.

The Dresden story, the Trail of Tears, Wounded Knee. Black Hawk's crossing, where they shot the grandmothers and the children as they floundered, tried to cross the river and sank into the netherworld, sown like seeds into the dark.

rise over the pass and the plains of mining . . . the tombs of the miners.

I thought she said, "The tombs of my grandfathers."

She gripped her bag and shook her head. She seemed excited, her face terrible, lifted in some memory, the blood-drenched earth, monster births and angels. "They hunted me, pierced me. I fled them down the dark. I fled them. I foxed them . . . they didn't take anything from me. I return . . . I laugh . . ."

And she laughed a terrible sound.

Her head dropped over the strange bag covered with roses as if she had been hanged.

We drove over those curved hills, over the Indian bodies, over the buried nuclear warheads now ready for the final massacre.

It all seemed below us. We skimmed across the top and the bus driver whistled "Amazing Grace" and flashed his lights off and on at buses coming from the opposite direction and seemed to get pleasure hitting rabbits that fled across his path.

I sat, gripped to myself as if she was a lens of some kind through which I saw the earth, the great seized ranch occupied by white hunters, and then entering the slag, the turned-over mutilated earth of the mines.

And I panicked.

I was wide awake now. I saw the town occupied by the state militia and Rockefeller's Pinkertons and armed mine guards, trying to keep the people out after the killing of the children . . . there must have been rumors going in all directions. My uncles in Kansas started out with their rabbit guns to defend their brother miners.

The desperate dead untethered in their time as in some drunken harvest sit pale against the taverns in the corn field and tell again the journey and praise the old hunters . . . praise the great fish and bison and the women and warriors opened to them, their generosity of flesh and loin . . . there are granaries where their potent seed is held for a good season. They grow huge with sacks of testicles of seed in the moonlight. Mist on the evening earth you pass them, hold your skirts tight to your knees, great earth ship full of dead men and women plowing the earth waves, surveyors and navigators, steer and stir the prow hair rises, woodpecker, cock entwined with grape leaves farther blue.

At Laguna the uranium mine cast a shadow on all the land and the ancient humans upon it. "Why he treated me like a slave," the dying Indian said, spitting up black stuff. "They pushed us back into the mine after they blasted. . . . I can't breathe here and I can't go someplace else. This has been my home for centuries. Blast and dust over our ancient villages. They gave us the radioactive slag to build our houses with. I am a slave of death."

The rays of the moon seemed to search the very bottom of the profound gulf; but still I could make out nothing distinctly on account of a thick mist in which every thing there was enveloped, and over which there hung a magnificent rainbow, like that narrow and tottering bridge which Musselman says is the only pathway between Time and Eternity.[10]

They came over the hills right through the guards, right through the loaded and pointed rifles. It was cold in the fall light, they were stopping all the trains, watching for Mother Jones who was going to deliver the graveside sermon for Tikas. The miners had brought his body to Trinidad.

If you ever drew into this funeral whirlpool of a communal ceremonial, you would never forget it . . . the appropriate, the real history coming from the event, the exploitation, the appearance, the opening of this century plant of workers' grief and passion. The hankering after the pure desire, and the freed passion of the body faced by murder, thrust of all contagion, infection, violence. The air bristling and threatening and pouring at last in communal grief. The immense anguish dying in the air in which we have to live.

"You told me," the young woman said clearly, leaning over to the bus driver, "that you would let me off outside Denver." He did not answer and she repeated it.

"You better just sit quiet," he threatened, "just shut your mouth and go where your ticket says, Denver."

"Denver's been blown up," she said, "all those bombs buried in her went off."

The white woman gasped . . . the skiers were sound asleep. "You better let me help you in Pueblo," she said. "Clean up a bit . . . you must have some clean clothes in your bag."

The girl turned her terrible face back and she hissed, "You mind your own business. It's no business of yours.

"Look ahead, driver, there's a narrow bridge . . . look ahead, take care, beware, there's a woman in the road

We are our own geography, the level of valley and hill, web of flesh. We are cemeteries in which the women lie buried and sometime reappear. She will reappear. I know that. Child of old woman.

Dusty and ghostly hair of the women killed covering their children in the pits of Ludlow. And then burned beyond recognition, but they rise in their memories. Press their remembered faces in the strange grief of this valley.

With Ludlow, seeing the pile of women in the newspaper, children and women piled like slaughterhouse meat. Dead child of mother bomb, child of uranium mercury poisoning. We are linked now. She moves toward me. Her resistance leaves, my walls go down. A link between us.

The district attorney of Colorado spoke at the League of Women Voters. The underground test posed no problem. It was monitored, controlled, would absolutely hurt nothing. It seemed that we all needed, everyone needs, one atomic test. Our security depends on it. Everything, every question is answered. The gate is shut, the fences are built. . . . We believed it. We trusted it.

Rosa De Anda

"You must not—you shall not behold this!" said I, shuddering, to Usher, as I led him, with a gentle violence, from the window to a seat. "These appearances, which bewilder you, are merely electrical phenomena not uncommon—or it may be that they have their ghastly origin in the rank miasma of the tarn."[11]

asking you to stop. Stop. Stop!" she cried. "There's a woman signaling you." He swerved . . . he saw her. . . .

"You can go so low you are free underneath. You can choose your death, not accept theirs. Don't let them give you death . . . only one to a person," she said.

"I told you," the bus driver said, "that this is a piece of road like nothing I ever seen. I can't in no way account for anything. See now, there's not just mist but it whirls and looks like people running or stopping the bus. Once an old man stood right in front of the headlights signaling something. I put on the brakes but I went right through that old man. No, sir."

He turned his face halfway toward us so I saw one eye roll back in a kind of terror. And he leaned toward the windshield, shading his eye and turning the wheel suddenly, erratically. And the mist did seem to have body, rose and fell, swirled away in the lights, and then we saw the desolate country toward Ludlow, with the mines on the left where the soldiers shot steadily into the tent colony of the striking miners after they had been evicted from the mining towns where they lived. The mists disappeared sometimes and I didn't see the sign of the Ludlow memorial to the Ludlow victims put up by the Mine Workers Union.

"There's a deer," he cried. "Why do they stand in the light, or was it a deer?"

The big white woman said loudly, "We are just going on the road to Pueblo, that's all . . . in a misty night . . . you are making things up."

"No, ma'am," he said. "Why, once a bus tipped clean

My husband was a geologist. It didn't make him see. We raised sheep for meat and wool. We had a ranch house. Very comfortable. What you will do for comfort. He saw the landscape but he didn't know they would bury the women live.

I had my womb cut out, scraped away, the center knifed away. So I would be empty forever. Radiation has life spans. They tell you different. They lied to us deliberately, knowing full well. They lied.

Even my husband who defended it cried out with his last breath, "Yes, they lied to us."

But in five years he died a terrible death of the radiated lung. Lost his job with the computers. Lost the ranch. Lost his son. Left me alone. Lost, lost. Go into the lost body, the lost country.

They said it was safe. What you need is an underground blast. Everything seems to shift. . . . Imagine blasting inside the heart, inside the womb, the liver, the pancreas, opening up the continent, opening up the pilgrim. Cut them open and give them a new heart, somebody else's heart. Open and pass into each other.

Mothers burst out of the tide of mass graves. Purloined light and overturned grave of earth, ghosts and skeletons, bones and marrow upturned, ripped open, great sharks of memory swimming in the vast sea night. Roar, emptiness, body snatched from the earth, grave bones burnt with coal. . . .

over right along here as if living hands tipped it as it ran."

"Nonsense," she said, "don't let him scare you."

"We are not afraid," I said. "My grandma was killed in the black hole of Ludlow."

"No kiddin'," he said.

"No kiddin'," I said.

Then the girl said clearly, "Don't hog the road, driver, let the people through. You're going too fast. No use getting to Denver, the explosion already was there . . . released all the gas stored there underground.

"Go slow now, driver, you're passing the fields where they sprayed her, go slow now, driver, for the little children killed by Mr. Rockefeller.

"Go slow and let the little children pass. They are going to the Judgment, the witnesses against him. Bring him to judgment all over the earth."

"My lands," the white woman said, "this is ridiculous . . . a bunch of lunatics."

The road seemed to be drawing us into a spectral world, into a landscape more real than the present . . . more remembered. We seemed to part the dark, a turbulent spectral dark on both sides, and then the headlights seemed to be unreal and like a deep sea, dense and clearing and then closing, as if the air through which we penetrated was the body of hundreds of ghosts running alongside us.

"Goddag," the bus driver cried, "there's a terrible wind. You got to have power to go through it. Holding us back . . . goddag it."

Mothers and babies were crucified on the altar of human liberty, the crucifixion was effected by the operators, paid gunmen, the dead will go down in history as the heroes, victims, the burnt offerings laid on the altar. Rockefeller, great god, greed, eight-hour day, narrow and dead, narrow and dead work. Fresh new grave.

I sat there in terror out of all proportion, my body was hot as hers glowing, something was falling into me, heating me . . . burning and illumination . . . I saw everything by this parturient light. Falling, glowing from another dimension, lighting the plains. The plains hung over us.

There were arabesque figures with unsuited limbs and appointments. There were delirious fancies such as the madman fashions. . . . And these—the dreams—writhed in and about, taking hue from the rooms, and causing the wild music of the orchestra to seem as the echo of their steps.[12]

It grew louder—louder—*louder!* And still
the men chatted pleasantly, and smiled.
Was it possible they heard not? Almighty
God!—no, no! They heard!—they sus-
pected!—they *knew!*—they were making a
mockery of my horror! [13]

We leaned forward, looking out the front window as
if we drove through a fissure opening before us, as if we
might plunge through the fissure of a quake, summoned
by some spectral ghost. It was a cadaverous look of
pestilence on the mist that pressed against the windows, now lighted with a strange sulphuric light. A
hideous long entombed throng pressed us back, released
by our penetrating light, and then it seemed we plowed
through a night meadow of dead children lying amid
an angelic mist of prairie flowers.

She said, "I want to help them but I can't lay my
burden down."

"Set down," the driver shouted, so that one of the
skiers cried in alarm, "What's up?"

"I got the wind," he cried, ". . . could blow us off the
road." You could not see now. We seemed to be sur-
rounded by a thick turmoil of winded ghosts. "If I stop
they might force the doors open."

"Who?" cried the skiers. "Who?" one cried, rising in
the aisle.

"It's only the wind," the white woman said as she
half rose to meet him in the aisle. Her head struck the
top of the bus ceiling.

"Lady," he cried, battling with the steering wheel.
"Only the wind. Jesus, you should take this wheel,
lady. We're driving through a covey of angry corpses."

"Corpses," she cried, and the skier sat down heavily.

I seemed to see the white beard of my grandfather,
his arms raised and his eyes gleaming out of the mist.

"He ran clear to Trinidad to tell the union about the
massacre of the women and children."

*They have taken her, they have come and taken the
child, the great prairie mothers . . . the great mine
mothers in the center of turquoise, nothing forgotten for
the lost Persephone, returns to bring back spring . . .
takes flowers to the underground, the spectres, the
sacred ghosts. We must have them. We must ask them
to our tables, our beds, our festivals. There is a void
without them.*

*Sunflowers thick in the Spanish meadows all spring
from empty eyes and bone, vessels spring to our vision
are part of our seeing. Their great golden whorl tender
as a mother's eye above the breast. It is all tender.
Knows you. Feeds you.*

Free ride, give us a free ride.

*All this womb torn open for coal and to make a
golden dome.*

"When was that?" the skier said.

"They're on something," the tall white woman said, "they're crazy. I am going to call the ambulance in Pueblo."

"Sit down, for Christ's sake," he said. "I can't drive straight here. You might fall and sue us."

She sat down.

I looked back and I saw them dead. I had heard about what Mother Jones had said at the funeral, "Never forget your fellow workers, those who died for you." But I had . . . I had forgotten. They make you disremember, forget, dismember. Remember . . . remember.

The driver knew, he made mad signals to the buses and trucks we passed, but they signaled back jovially and drove on in the opposite direction.

Something opens in the night . . . the land . . . the body . . . and I know that she also had been here in her memory and flesh.

She was pressed against the window.

"It's Colorado," she said. "My grampa is buried in the hill. My gramma running with the dead child after she cut the cord like me, it come down easy," she said, "like a knife of vengeance . . . angel of death."

"Watch out, driver," she cried suddenly, leaning toward him with a face like Medusa. "Watch out. They'll wreck you, they'll get you. They'll turn the bus over." She fell back to press against the window.

"There they are," she said, "there they are . . . my gramma running with a dead baby . . . there she is, gramma, gramma . . . I come back to you . . . your dead baby revenged . . . yes, a witness . . . bear witness. They say . . ."

Share your death with me. Break the bread of death. Break bread and drink my sacred blood, mingle it with yours, let me not fear.

I flash on her life. Small, bent in the fields with her grandmother dying of the poisonous spray used on the insects. See her beat to the ground, thrust under, taken it is called. She was taken. Fleeing the back roads from field to field. Not enough to keep the slave alive. I see her pursuer, the smell of the killer. The mystery of human seed seized by conquerors.

The sorrow and agony of the valley . . . sorrow, the mad dead with justice in them.

There seemed to be a howling and the engine answered, the driver leaned over the wheel peering into the whirling ghosts.

"It's true they came to kill you." Her face was white as the howling ghosts against the pane . . . her mouth was open as if screaming.

The bus was dim, the skiers sleeping, the night opened, extending space, changed, was occupied. We were moving through and into one another. No barriers, no skin, all fell open in us . . . bright levels alive in the hills, in the dark, began to flow, put down in ancient memory. And I heard the sound of the miners coming out of the mines, thousands who crept underground, pouring down to the open grave.

I didn't see the sign that says "Ludlow," that invites you to go to the monument, put up by the Mine Workers Union . . . a woman angel, her sword over the dead and guarding the children. And there is a cellar door over the hole of the massacre, you can go down into the dark. The glow of bones in the pit of the massacre, the bones of the children glowing, something concave bends over the edge.

"Rabbits," he said, "they love the lights."

"Don't," she cried, "God will punish you."

"For rabbits?"

"For pain," and she hung her head down, the black straight hair over her face.

Then suddenly we seemed to enter another world, rise out of the strange holocaust, we rose along the Rockies now, those old mountains, toward the steel mills of Pueblo.

. . . the interior of an immensely long and rectangular vault or tunnel, with low walls, smooth, white, and without interruption or device. Certain accessory points of the design served well to convey the idea that this excavation lay at an exceeding depth below the surface of the earth. No outlet was observed in any portion of its vast extent, and no torch or other artificial source of light was discernible; yet a flood of intense rays rolled throughout, and bathed the whole in a ghastly and inappropriate slumber.[14]

Don't open the door—the driver says they will try to stop the bus. Never seen anything like it. The distorted face at the window, the toothless mouth begging you to speak. Let them in. Let them in.

We are the minute, we survive the fire. We are the protein . . . something unusable, indestructible.

Don't laugh, there is something more powerful than you know. It is in the tiniest, the smallest corn kernel and smaller than that. The human kernel can endure for fifty thousand years waiting for heat and moisture, terrible story of begetting and birth.

A strange quiet . . . the bus drove through now, the
road clear and simple, leading ahead clearly, with little
ranches, and cattle looking up out of the mountain
night.

All the skiers were asleep now, and the woman sat
belligerent, watching, waiting.

"It's still an hour from Pueblo," the driver said. "Take
it easy, but take it. Goddag, it's good to be able to see,
back on the track. Never saw the like of it.

"Danged funny," the bus driver said, "I swan, I can't
account for it. From now to Pueblo it's a breeze. Those
danged thick ghostly . . . no accounting for it. If I was
superstitious. . . . Was a terrible thing, though, any way
you look at it. Shootin' down into the place they dug for
their children. The mining company, Mr. Rockefeller.

"Why, Mr. Rockefeller was one of the great men . . .
foundation . . . his family now has international power
. . . you know, he made America."

I was shaken. I felt when you begin to remember,
they come up out of the living mist.

If I should forget thee O Jerusalem. . . .

I felt I was waiting for something.

*The ruined gutted and raped land, imaged with women
. . . the labor leached from the body . . . violets out of
the slag pits . . . the qualities that rise, delicate beauty
and strength, generosity . . . the true American earth
rising out of the destruction.*

Out of my sleep I woke with horror, touched by her
hand. She was leaning toward me smiling, nodding
and smiling in some awful happiness.

"This is the key," she said, and between her calloused
fingertips of a picker she held a tiny key, between her
thumb and finger. "This is the key," she said. "Do you

*It begins softly in us, like corn and wheat, one kernel
of protein falls to be nurtured by us all.*

But these intervals of tranquility are only at the turn of the ebb and flood, and in calm weather, and last but a quarter of an hour, its violence gradually returning.[15]

want to see?"

"No," I whispered. The bus was dark now, and all asleep, even the white woman snored lightly.

"Don't you want to see what I have?"

"Not now," I said. "Better sleep. Sleep a little. You need sleep."

"I don't need sleep," she said. "You want to see how great, how wonderful? You want to see?"

She leaned her white face forward and her fetid breath came into my nostrils and I drew back in horror.

"He killed me. He was an expert marksman. The goal, the target, the quick deed, the eviction, the end of a ten-hour day . . . thirty cents a basket . . . fifty cents an hour. Also stuff taken off . . . meals . . . sometimes got nothing . . . paid the coyote."

I couldn't look at her in that light. She seemed dead. Kabuki color of suicide, bile pallor, chemical bitten bare, something hemorrhaging out of her . . . fright of her blood, she wiped her face with the green rag. Tore at her flesh as if wiping it off the bone . . . pallor that was chemical . . . some bitter odor of acid blood came from her . . . the woman was sniffing it. Was it cocaine? I saw again her tennis shoe with a torn hole in it. She was very strangely pale . . . like a woman stirring a burning pot in a huge fire . . . the terrible sulphuric glow lit in her.

She smiled and drew close.

The white woman was snoring . . . the dead lay all around us, the great heads of the skiers out of the sulphuric dark.

She rose out of the dark plains, the glass window reflected only the dead in the bus . . . she seemed to

My flesh is your flesh said the corn. . . . Prayer for white corn, mother, empty stomach and pain, life-giving powers . . . to be fed . . . feed my sheep . . . our mother has been seated among us . . . the bride has been in the lilacs . . . the matron is dreaming in the squash blossom when she will be full and round containing summer . . . Persephone is leading them up and out, up the stem to the flowering summer she comes, out of this bright cold green from hell.

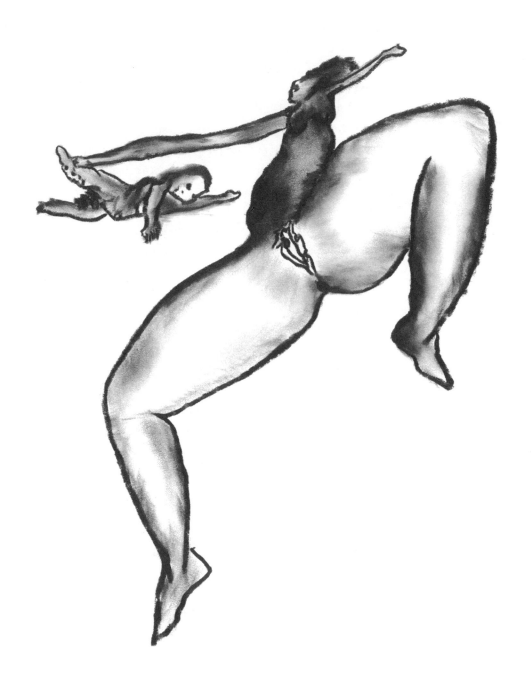

Rosa De Anda

flame and weave in some strange air . . . she put her hands upon the bag as if to release something. I didn't want to see. I couldn't run. Stop the bus, I wanted to cry, as she had cried . . . let me out . . . the bus driver looked back uneasily, but he also was dead in the dreadful journey.

Something dark on her hand like dried blood . . . and between her bloodied fingers she raised, showed me, held in front of me, the tiny key . . . no bigger than her fingernail.

I was dumbly shaking my head. "No, no". . . she put her finger to her lips and looked at the sleeping corpses reflected in the glass coffin.

"Yes," she said, a smiling woman who had just made something beautiful. She put the tiny key into the lock covered by a flap with a painted rose on it and she reached over and began to unzip the bag slowly, looking delightful and secret, smiling. Watching the sleeping woman in the seat behind, she lifted half of the unzipped cover and I could not help looking unless I was stricken blind. And to my horror I saw a tiny shrunken dark face, like those shrunken heads, ceremonials of some hunters. . . . It was her face and her straight black hair stuck out of a knitted blue cap. The rest of the body was in a knit snowsuit you buy at the five and dime with feet and mittens part of it. His swollen eyes were closed and he was dead.

She was smiling secretly, triumphantly, to show me the savior of the world, for the three wise men, for the morning star to sing aloud.

"Look," she whispered, and took off the blue knit cap releasing the long black hair and the curious tiny

—I'll give you a riddle.
It will never die in the beet fields.
It will never fight a war for the powerful.
It will go live with its grandmother.
The field boss won't crack the whip.
It won't cross any border, go down in any mine.

Round head coming down in the El Paso women's room . . . yes, perfect nobody helped me he came out perfect . . . he is not dead, but risen from the foul sprays . . . from the enemies, he can bear witness what they do . . . he can rise in the light and never grow old . . . dead he speaks for us all . . . the dead children rise in him.

replica of her face and straight black hair.

I didn't see it . . . it appeared to me as a burning bush. There was no object. It was an icon, already hallowed, already with meaning . . . and the old eyes, half opening in voluptuous half sight of a prophet or of a tortured person. Only the mouth looked childlike, as if regretting not finding the nipple, never to suck a breast of earth.

I changed forever . . . never to think again, I didn't think . . . it was the image of death rendered at the placenta, at the wound of birth . . . at once and deliberate. . . .

The earth, the road, the place of instant death and crucifixion, this was no promise, no illusion, no lie . . . this was the final and true image. No ambiguities, no double vision, no hesitation, no controversy . . . it was instant, clear, absolute. The bond in our own breast and womb . . . in our flesh, in the body, in the blood.

"He is dead." Question or declaration? Is he dead? Who is dead? She smiled, put her hand around his head no bigger than an apple. "They did not kill him," she said. "They tried to kill him . . . they all knifed him . . . he was killed when they poisoned my grandmother. You see, I gave him his own death . . . the liberty of his own death, out of my grandmother. My dead mother couldn't breathe what they sprayed on us like bugs. I kept him, I ran with him . . . I gave him our own death . . . liberty or death . . . that's it, liberty or death. Gave him his pure, his own death, not a terrible life. I chose for him. He's perfect, see. I had a perfect, dead child."

As I rapidly made the mesmeric passes, amid ejaculations of "dead! dead!" absolutely *bursting* from the tongue and not from the lips of the sufferer, his whole frame at once—within the space of a single minute, or even less, shrunk—crumpled—absolutely *rotted* away beneath my hands.[17]

This child runs into us, through us. We are not watching it at a distance. There is no distance now. Everything takes place inside. The dead child swimming through her. I have no choice now, there are not two sides. There is only one side. The child.

—It is not cruel to die. It is cruel to live.

The ash of grandmothers. Ignite, under the ashes, begot on old fires. Believe the fire is still burning under the ash of continents, the fire of the oppressed. What is underneath has been saved. What is suppressed, hidden, there is something immense in the smallest. It is in the most minute that the savior lives.

She was leaning into him. "Cry. Cry. Salt him like a king of Egypt in our earth, pyramids filled with the corpses of our fathers and mothers. The great pyramids of the Rockies . . . in the sacred mounds of the earth . . . give, let us have our own death . . . a warning . . . a revenge . . . he won't be a cheap worker for Mr. Rockefeller or a beet puller being sprayed. Will he? He'll be a witness for all ages. A witness for our Lord . . . for our grands and great grands . . . you see . . . I thought you'd see . . . now you are a witness. Now you can spread the news about those who choose their own death."

I've heard of captured people who won't breathe . . . have no one coming into bondage . . . pass away . . . pass out.

"You see?"

"Yes," I nodded . . . among the dead no one stirred. I thought the driver was dead, but he turned uneasily. He wanted to see what was in the bag. Her light fell on us, and the dead light of the child amongst our dead . . . the change, the transformation. The death that makes you endure could have grown flowers in the night bus.

"He looks like gramma, she suffered awful, her body with the cancer-poison given her by the companies. Her eyes didn't close like that, kept looking accusing. 'I accuse you.' I had to put a penny on 'em. Thought my eyes were being stitched shut forever but she told me to look . . . she said, 'Don't do it, daughter, look what they are doing, look, point, accuse, show, cry out.' That's her last words, my gramma, stooped all her life in them fields, all over this land . . . all over."

The face of love rises in marriage, work, assemblage; like the interlocking tones of a sweet song, love does not come visiting, love is forged and we are forging it.

This is our child. We ate his blood in our fruit. We used his body in our vegetables. This is our child, perfect and embodying the death we gave him. This is our death . . . touch it, run with it, lift it up in the domes of gold.

To us wounded the glad child comes. That this land is ours, our labor is ours, our seed is strong. The people are arriving. The wail of infants of ravaged terrain, landscape seethes with light, we rise. We rise with the corn and wheat.

They blind, deafen, and strangle you, and take away all power of action or reflection. But we were now, in a great measure, rid of these annoyances—just as death-condemned felons in prison are allowed petty indulgences, forbidden them while their doom is yet uncertain.[18]

I longed yet dared not to employ my vision. I dreaded the first glance at objects around me. It was not that I feared to look upon things horrible, but that I grew aghast lest there should be *nothing* to see. At length, with a wild desperation at heart, I quickly unclosed my eyes. My worst thoughts, then, were confirmed.[19]

She whispered, "Don't let them take me in Pueblo. He that got it on me tried to knife it outa me. 'Abort, abort,' they cried, and I run. I run day and night. I run from them to keep him myself. Don't let them take us at Pueblo or Denver."

I turned my full self to her in wonder and terror.

She had run in the ladies' room at El Paso alone, carrying that strange seed without a cry . . . on the toilet . . . catching the wizened head, she cut the cord . . . she was smiling now, showing me a knife, nodding, "I did it," she said, "myself. I am powerful. I am good. I am capable. I had a whole and entire, perfect child."

Remember the girl in Nazi Germany with her baby, they split the village at the crossroads. One road went to the left, went to instant death, the other went to the work in a factory . . . death later . . . the girl and her baby were sent to the left. They did not believe her . . . put her in an asylum later, then found out it was true. Everyone who went to the left was killed. She was under a heap of corpses. She could not find her dead baby. Got out, came back to the village.

I never remember how we got to Pueblo. I thought I heard her whispering, telling her whole life. I knew it. I saw them stooping in the fields after the men were blacklisted at Ludlow, thrown to the edge of the country, native aliens driving at night from field jobs, I saw them on a dark screen thrown on my flesh. I read it from the vast dread road we followed. This baby could not be simply dead like naked birds thrust out of feathered nests.

We were not supposed to survive. We were not supposed to be here. They thought they had killed us all. Touch us, we are here. Pain is fertile, nurtures the communal spirit within.

The carrion rots into fields of wheat, the battlefields grow men again in bread and protein. What they do in making death rots and makes crops again. They cannot help it. The road is toward bread. The will is to life, conception springs from decay, from murder, rape, mayhem. The inclination is fiery toward form and being and brightness. We move among each other, arrive at harvest in the midst of holocaust.

I felt awkward, anguished, next to her and saw her hands. The dark scabs were blood.

I received her fierce message. We could not leave him to rot, he was a witness. He must be seen, it must be seen how his death was justice. How he rose from the black hole of Ludlow and the poison of the fields and the indignity of hunger and exile in his own country. Yes, he had died to make us free. I felt that clearly. I felt fierce for his defense now, in the dark dread of this night road.

I leaned close to her and said, "I'll get a dress and you can change." She shook her head. "When we get off at Pueblo you can change."

"No," she said.

"I'll get off and keep the woman from phoning. She's a bloodhound." Her eyes widened in fear.

We rose into the mountains. The earth had a ridge of illumination around it turning into dawn, with the flush of a mother as if we went smiling now into her.

The driver was quiet. Able to see clearly now.

The white woman sat rigid, watching.

She leaned over once and said, "You know the seat goes back, just press on the arm underneath."

We didn't answer her or appear to hear her.

Something had changed. Light entered the bus like the fuzz on a peach.

The girl sat up straight, reflected in the mirror, her arms easy with love over the bag. Once she gently put it on my lap and we smiled together.

We sat next to each other. Why did her appearing reveal everything? As if we struck light into each other. Entered the earth wound. With the earth we drove through the terrible wound. My son visible. My husband dead. The comfort gone, the house gone, the land gone. The hundreds of dead, torn out, deformed blotched eyes, lambs lying tender in their curled fur, dead, dropped dead out of the grieving ewes. The ewes went mad. Some ran away bawling. Something had struck them at the axis of their being.

The night chant of the Navajo. The night chant of the mountains going to Denver. The earth appears . . . rises. This is the resurrection and the life.

I did not die. I did not give myself to madness. I shall not leave you. Sometimes I think they did not hear me at all.

He who has never swooned is not he who finds strange palaces and wildly familiar faces in coals that glow; is not he who beholds floating in midair the sad visions that the many may not view. . . .[20]

She burned next to me. I felt strange, as if I had changed, something coming in density and force in me . . . about to be embodied or spoken. She had struck into me like a meteor, landing deep within me, fire and blood. I put my hand over her on the rose secret, as if we knew what to do after years of blindness.

We lifted easy into the coming light which seemed like balm on a terrible sore. It poured like milk from the east, just a rose rim of flowing light. The terrible sulphur heat seemed to die down in her like a fire and I thought she was asleep till I heard her whispering, "Don't let them get me now. I had to run from their knife, their danger. 'Take it out, take it out,' he said. He had scissors, burnt a coat hanger to kill the germs . . . they suction it out. They said, 'The best thing.' Pierce you, take away everything. . . ." I didn't turn my head. I looked down at our hands clasped on the big red roses. "He is perfect now. I had him now . . . in our own death . . . we got our own death . . . and alone we had each other. He is a witness now. They'll never get his life. No stoop labor, they call it. Don't stoop now. I bore this witness to death as you, Lord . . . not my will . . . you want to see him once more?" she leaned, smiling.

"No, no, she's watching." She nodded, smiling.

"I don't think there will be cops in Pueblo," I said.

"You don't?"

I felt the woman peering over the seat. "What is that smell?"

The pull, I hold her, I am astonished terrible excited like a meadow in the rain (terrible not to be touched), I am like a greening meadow in the rain and thousands of flowers. I am deep, silent, excited, wide awake, the light strikes the sheer cliff of stone and the desert foliage and manzanita.

And her dark head, I put my hand into her hair that falls down. I forget how warm another human being is. I feel wonder, embarrassment, vast silence of mountains waiting.

His tongue cut out, his hands and feet all touch and recognition. Let him speak, let me hold him up, not hide him. It has not been written down. It must be told. It must be seen. We must know it.

I set forthwith, and with entire deliberation, to the task of concealing the body. I knew that I could not remove it from the house, either by day or by night, without the risk of being observed by the neighbors.[21]

"A rat," I said. "Funny smeller you have."

"Well, it's pretty sharp," she said. "I been in this business for twenty years and I can spot something needing investigation."

"Well, we'll soon be in Denver and it will be over."

"What will be over? It's never over . . . these girls are everywhere in trouble, dangerous . . . it's my duty . . . excuse me, I am going to phone."

I leaned against her. "Oh, it's been too much, all the suspicion about that girl . . . I think it's just crazy . . . you got an aspirin?"

"A good American can't refuse an aspirin," she fumbled in her bag.

I decided not to let her call Denver. I would watch her every minute.

"Help me," the girl said.

"I'm with you always," I said. "We are together. I'll see she doesn't phone or call the cops or the social workers."

She squeezed my hand. We began to come into Pueblo, past the big mills and the state asylum.

I wasn't afraid now.

"Ten minutes," the driver said, "we'll be in Pueblo. Fifteen minutes, folks, and we take this same bus out for Denver. Those changing, going to Kansas, Missouri, Oklahoma . . ."

"You sure," the woman said, "you don't want to get off? Wash and a change of clothing?"

She stood there a moment with the skiers behind her.

"All right, Mrs., we got to get a drink here. Fifteen minutes."

I remember after the massacre there was a terrible passion to get the bodies. Don't let the children fall into their hands. Don't let the mothers, the women, the wives, fall into their murderous hands. To get the bodies out of there to Trinidad on that terrible night.

For many hours the immediate vicinity of the low framework upon which I lay had been ,literally swarming with rats. They were wild, bold, ravenous—their red eyes glaring upon me as if they waited but for motionlessness on my part to make me their prey. "To what food," I thought, "have they been accustomed in the well?"[22]

"Oh, Girlie, you still got that bag of Mary and Juan, I bet."

"All right, folks," the driver said, "fifteen minutes. Remember your bus number. Don't want to leave you."

I went down the steps ahead of the woman.

"What's the matter with her, driver?" she asked.

"Oh, she just had a little too much in El Paso, I guess. She ain't hollering or nothing."

"Come on," I said to her, "let's get some coffee."

I took her arm boldly. I hated the feel of her. She drew away. "There's the bus cops," she said. "I'll talk to them."

I kept hold of her. "They're going to search the bus again," she said. "They'll spot her as something wrong."

"Oh, why should they?" I said. "You saw she had papers for the border cops. . . .

"Let's get some coffee. I should get change."

"I got change," she said. "I come prepared."

I kept trying to see the bus. The doors cut off my sight. Then I saw the cops coming out.

"I'll have time to phone," she said. "I can have my assistant meet us and take her to a doctor."

"You're a social worker," I said.

"We've got five minutes," she said, holding out her huge gaunt hand. She turned from me, starting for the phones, a row of them along the wall in glass cases. I ran toward her. I don't know what I intended, certainly not to hurt her. I ran into her, injecting my foot between her ankles and she fell so easily, crumpling to the floor.

Two women stopped. I bent over her. She was like a fallen tree, hard bark in pieces as if I had to put her

We are all dead in the bus in the poisoned night. The plains are burning, the nuclear bombs underground in Nevada, the chemical gas buried in Colorado . . . released, gone. We are gone. A glass coffin going to a mass grave . . . cities blown into the mother air, coming down slow.

together some way, and I wanted to laugh and I tried to tug at her. She seemed a solid harsh weight.

"You bitch," she hissed. "You did that on purpose."

The driver came out of the office. "Are you hurt?" he said, taking hold of her on the other side.

He began to swipe at her skirt and she drew away.

"I'm all right," she said. "Will I have time to phone?"

"No," he said. "I'm just about to announce the bus. We're a little late. We'll be in Denver before you have time to say Jack Robinson. Everybody on his toes." The skiers slowly got on the bus and I saw the girl's face at the window and she was waving at me and smiling.

I sat down and she tenderly put the bag across my knees.

She looked triumphant and smiling.

There were wet marks on her blouse.

Her milk had come in.

Milk for the messiah, I thought. Milk for the dead witness.

Everything had changed. It was strange . . . the light seemed now a loving substance, beckoning arms outspread as if we went through her rich body, the body of the earth which now opened before us, embracing us, gathering us in, offering us light and milk. Grief seemed assuaged but not forgotten, and the ghosts of the multitudinous dark seemed now penetrated by the vast light of the planet, and the road seemed to rise out of the great dread into this coming light.

I had never felt this way before. Some terrible anxiety in my breast came into tears.

She was alone, she was glorious in the chemical dark, she had nothing but herself and her glowing. She and the decay, the phosphorous light of decay. . . . Born out of this womb of violence, struggle, she fought for him. He was dead at Ludlow, shot at in the earth where they hid their children under the tents.

Wherever I am I can do this. I am this. End canticle of the earth, indestructible. This is what you mean by mother. The mother essence, which is energy indestructible unusable undiminished unspendable. You cannot spend her strength or use it up or poison it. . . . Our mother did not know she was defeated. She did not know she was doomed, stricken, tramped down. She had no way of admitting or entertaining this concept. She never expected to be a rose.

There was blood upon her white robes, and the evidence of some bitter struggle upon every portion of her emaciated frame. For a moment she remained trembling and reeling to and fro upon the threshold. . . .[23]

I put my hand over her two bloody hands gripping the bag and she lifted her face like a meteor. It struck into me. She turned her cold hands upward and gripped mine. Her belly seemed to emit a terrible heat . . . a fire burning, and her seed-sown crop of the oppressed . . . tread the seed down and the heat of the milk coming for the dead messiah.

"He's beautiful," she said. "They did not think I could make anything like him. They wanted to pierce me. Now, he is witness to their cruel killing. You will tell about him and he will show the death of poison in the field . . . he looked like my gramma . . . you take his little blue cap."

"Oh, no," I said. "Yes, I will take it. Yes, I will."

Our hands gripped as we rapidly mounted in the coming dawn toward Denver.

I took her hot hand. I held it tight. She was patting the bag and smiling. "He's perfect, just perfect. They thought I couldn't have anything perfect . . . he's perfect . . . he's a witness for my Lord . . . he's a witness for my grampa."

I pulled her down. I stroked her. I took the bag across my knees. I drew her head onto my shoulder. I crooned to her. I wanted to pour my being into her.

"They didn't get me," she said. "I fooled them all." She was leaning close to me, whispering to me and I felt her terrible fever and odor of blood.

The dead child strikes into us, into our skin . . . we won't bury him and forget him as you did Ludlow. They will never stop screaming, appearing stricken, covering their smashed heads, the myriad holes you blasted in their bodies. They will howl and shriek. You will not sleep. You cannot live.

Her presence is communal. She came out of the communality, came out from between her legs from the lips, the double axe.

In your detail of the vision which presented itself to you amid the hills, you have described, with the minutest accuracy, the Indian city of Benares, upon the Holy River. The riots, the combats, the massacre, were the actual events of the insurrection of Cheyte Sing, which took place in 1780. . . .[24]

"Oh, I did it myself, alone," she said. "And I brought the afterbirth for my grandmother. I got it in a cellophane bag. My grandmother said the umbilical cord is your line of life and you can always come back to your gramma and she'll show you the way if you're lost."

"Let's cover him," I whispered, feeling the breath of the white woman as she leaned to listen. I didn't fear her now. I felt illumined in the destruction. Death is your only free dignity of choice . . . your retort . . . give me liberty or give me death.

In my closed hand I gave her back her little knife . . . and she winked at me and I saw the awful burden on her back from carrying potato sacks short-weighed.

I let them put him away and deny their guilt and I have not accused them . . . I have entered their conspiracy . . . I let them make me hide him and not testify at the trials. I dishonored him. I betrayed him and all the children dead upon the earth.

"Put the knife away," I said. I heard the sound of them slitting the throat of an angel.

Now we fled together with this cold witness . . . the dreaming child . . . this poisoned bird. The land was not dead, not acid, not a corpse, it was a witness now around us like this child illuminating the massacre, the terrible careless mass death.

I saw in the dark all over the world women running with their babies' corpses in their arms, running in bomb light, pursued by drawn bayonets to pierce them . . . your dead are holy.

I was thinking of hunger, long hours underground, false weight for your coal, the slow squeezing and dehydration of the body and the woman and the family, the children, slow starvation. America was grown also on hunger and terrible labor, deathly labor that you could not win. I was thinking of hunger and death . . . ten cents an hour . . . now I am thinking of hunger. Hunger is a form, an object, a presence, the sealed lips, the sealed mines, the sealed American silences.

The sweetest meanings of all we touch. Objects join us, the bread knife, the spider's web . . . the snake poison . . . the dark of herbal night and the smell of nightshade and poisonous sumac . . . come to our hands . . . the chairs befriend us, nuzzle us, take us with you . . . the hammock . . . the knife, the hammer, the awl . . . the brother and sister tools join us. Use me, bring me back, I am not a commodity, I am the extension of your loving labor.

What was to be always marked along the road. Road markers. Road runner. The image was from the future in America. Europe was wiped out. Unfallen titans of Atlantis rising under sea planted here all the time mountains rising over accumulation of privilege mass exploitation . . . prophetic even, all was prophesied daily in America. This was progress. The future all done for the children.

The bus drove into the accepting air, the earth seemed female, changing utterly and now alight and protecting us, curving around us. The white woman snored and seemed small. The skiers all fell into the aisles like dead men in a battle, hung from the chairs in the dark, silent, dead.

"Danger," she said, "drive carefully, driver. We have to get there. We have a message. Yes, a message."

Something broke like an egg, the earth egg, and in it we were with the women running with their mouths open in an awful scream, the children in Nicaragua drowned in the river . . . the howling faces of women, their dead children in their arms, death upon them from the sky, from enemies they never knew, holding the dead children, appearing everywhere, running, skin flailed, burnt off, skinless, awful death entering them. Now the children hang from the crosses, lie in the tombs dead from hunger. . . .

The tidal flesh rose from the flowered bag. There was no distance now. As if the earth like a thread came into us. We stopped at the railroad tracks, and I thought the great electric conduits were Tikas beckoning and holding out his arms to us and Mother Jones, her arms spread at the funeral to contain us all, and the cops striking her, that little woman. I zipped the bag open and in the dark we leaned over him and he looked different now. Tenderly taken down from the cross, he was not a child now but an icon of the dispossessed, of the brutally murdered, of the nuclear holocaust.

The great and terrible refineries and gas stations, the great impossible conduits of gas . . . electricity conducted over vast spaces, mountains . . . the great Kachina towers of the marking of this force, harnessed, stepped up in gigantic dynamos. Power carried and tossed into far cities . . . glow and grandeur of our achievement . . . crops of youth standing like abandoned fields . . . unsurveyed potentials . . . phantoms . . . obsolete human beings discarded . . . junk cities of humans.

The hurricane of women is simply moving forward, moving over you, something powerful is moving . . . in the hurricane it is said there is the work of workers for centuries, in one hurricane now the world of women rises and the predators can tremble and hide and run and die.

I became aware of a loud and gradually increasing sound, like the moaning of a vast herd of buffaloes upon the American prairie. . . . Even while I gazed, this current acquired a monstrous velocity. Each moment added to its speed—to its headlong impetuosity.[25]

For the first time during many hours—or perhaps days—I *thought*. It now occurred to me that the bandage, or surcingle, which enveloped me, was unique. I was tied by no separate cord.[26]

Who distanced us from the horror? Who killed him so we could be alienated from his death and seizure? The dead child lay on my knees now like my mutant son with no face. I had no fear now. I began to cleverly plan how we would evade the cops in Denver. How nothing could stop us. I felt strange, as if everything was closer and entered me, and nothing was alien, no suffering too horrible for me.

We were all inside together. Nothing could be denied or frightening. I said to her, "I am with you always . . ." and I saw the Pueblo steel mills and the raw open pits and the mutilated and screaming earth and my mutilated son rotting from nuclear emanations.

I was now a different woman. The earth had opened, a female passage before dawn. As if I rose out of the threat and silence of my life, rose toward all the imprisoned and dead children, toward my son, freed of the threat of the killers.

I could feel the woman behind me alert, awake, venomous.

I felt alert, sitting bolt upright, watching . . . ready to spring.

The girl was also alert. Her eyes closed and her bloody fingers gripping the zipper bag now, this birthing pouring from her . . . stirring rhythm in her emission of a being, rhythms of work and birth and death . . . the cord cut off, bleeding in the dead child, broken, torn off, the broken flesh fallen in her.

We entered the mountains that spread in the slowly rising light like the knees of the pieta holding the dead

Nothing is closed. All opens. No door, frontier wall of death. Speak woman, move, cut the strings of your tongue. They have sewed your eyes shut, poured water through your heart . . . denied the blood. The dogs are barking. The peddlers are coming to town, some in rags, some in tags, some in velvet gowns.

sons. We lay on her knees that spread with the grace of sorrow the death of the infant child . . . all the dead sons of the earth.

I understood about the dead child, already the corpse had illumined my life. I felt it clearly. I knew what I was going to do. I knew I had to do it.

How we are masked. How we are deadened. I am a college graduate, yet I can defile life like this. Blinded by an illusion entering a conspiracy of death without even knowing it. Forgetting the bodies of those ancestors, those miners, those great illuminators who received the human knowledge in the breast . . . I felt my whole body stir as if saved from death, returning from some awful necromancy. I felt a certain terrible happiness . . . as if at last I could accept the terrible distortions of my son and hold him to the earth and air as witness of some terrible evil that had been done to him . . . and to millions . . . a witness as she said . . . yes, a witness. I couldn't wait to gather up his lonely bones with his terrible eyes in his half-gone face . . . eyes always following me. Eyes from the body of Ludlow.

I could feel him drawing me to him, waiting for me to speak for him who would never speak. I would never hide him now.

"Denver in a few minutes," the driver said, and the bus stirred as he put on the top lights and the dark receded and the glass coffin lit and the corpses stirred . . . I had a wild confusion. You could not call a hospital . . . they would seize the child . . . dead in their province. Was she hemorrhaging? She was paler and I could not tell.

We are made out of labor on the flesh, hunger in the bowels, anger in the corn seed. We are entirely of it. Without any contention, we are simply going to pour over you. You are few, we are many, and we are just going to inundate you, drown you, save your lives from greed.

It begins inside, a tiny seed. It begins softly. The kernel is carried on the cob and cannot seed itself alone. It must be with others, nurtured by us all, kept green and alive. It begins with one, then two or three, then more, the country extends to stars. Softly they sustained us all. Multiplied on the communal cob it grew around the globe and is in starlight. The kernel has fallen into us all and taken root.

I saw clearly the doom that had been prepared for me, and congratulated myself upon the timely accident by which I had escaped. Another step before my fall, and the world had seen me no more.[27]

We were coming into Denver, the strange lights and streets, as if we landed from outer space. I put my hand over hers. She didn't respond. She was straining now, leaning forward, and I saw her face in the windshield and one eye of the bus driver in his rear mirror.

The bus driver was turning his head nervously and the white woman stirred and sat bolt upright out of a nightmare, and the girl put down the cover over the tiny corpse. But she was smiling victoriously at me, secretly, as if we had some triumph between us.

"We'll be in Denver in ten minutes," the bus driver didn't turn to look at us, "change for Minneapolis, Chicago, New York, and Peoria, St. Louis, San Francisco. This bus will end here. Take your belongings with you and find your schedules at the ticket office. Thank you for going Greyhound." His face showed anxiety as he turned to look at us . . . the white woman was getting ready to get her bag on the rack . . . the skiers turned sluggishly to get their equipment together, rising, startled out of the white light now coming into the bus from the mountain dawn . . . a sepulchral light showing no source yet, except as if coming from the corpse-like figures and from the unlit earth and space.

I helped her put on her imitation leather hat . . . she gripped the bag against her . . . she included me now in her look of excitement, pleading . . . "It's Okay," I said. "I'll keep her away . . . if the cops are there . . . I don't feel they will be."

"No," she said. "No, no. . . ." gripping the flowered bag.

You'll see me, she winks. I'll be there. I'll appear with him everywhere. Yes, keep an eye out. . . . I'll make my connection, don't worry, he is the connection. Don't worry, meet you in the golden bowl. The pitcher broken at the well.

The roads in America are becoming military roads, to Black Mesa, being amputated, cut up, cannibalized . . . to the place of the massacre, to the bones, to the skull of the buffalo, to the lonely cabin of the suicide. . . . The slow dread yearly wind-chilling legends, the shadows pouring down the dark side, the flight of arrows tipped with poison, couldn't get there because of the first inch, couldn't build a house for lack of an inch. The mustangs and the doomed burros join the buffalo. Celestial journeying. . . . Did you get the lay of the land. They are all barricaded in their rooms. As long as a widow's night.

"Just get out of the station as fast as you can."

It didn't occur to me to make a place where we could meet . . . as if we could not be separated now.

I gripped her hands . . . I put my arm around her shoulder. I met the awful glance of the white woman who now was standing in the aisle. I stood in front of her, barring her way, and helped hold the bag while the girl passed me and turned for the bag. The bus driver was waiting nervously for her at the bottom of the bus steps, but she would not let him take the bag. "Beat it," he said, searching the bus station behind him. I looked too. Not many people, some sleeping in the white dawn, looking like corpses too. No sign of cops. Standing in front of the white woman, I saw the girl half running through the station. The opaque glass doors let her through before I turned to the angered woman pressing against me. "Can I help you?" I said. I felt such a strange joy. "You're a bitch," she said in a low voice. "You are in cahoots. You're probably cocaine peddlers coming across the border . . . that's what was in the bag. I'll have you arrested as an accomplice."

I am an accomplice, I thought, for the rest of my life.

Yes, I went ahead of her down the steps, and the bus driver pressed my arm as if in a conspiracy. He knew something about her. She had gotten on the bus in El Paso. He had seen something, sensed something.

I waited with my baggage check and the white woman was nervous trying to point her bag out and then we saw them . . . two men in uniforms coming in the glass door looking around. "There they are," she said, grabbing her bag, . . . "don't let her get away," she said,

I personally aided . . . in the arrangements for the temporary entombment. The body having been encoffined, we two alone bore it to its rest.[28]

The gravid woman coming into milk, the plains, the memory, the corpse. She enters my vision. The growth of this horror in the eye. Her weird and fierce rejection of me, watching me. You're not an agent, she said, or a police woman. No, I said. A conduit, a nerve, a message down my nerves. Down which your angry body goes on a road, a journey, a terrible journey. A smile like an acre of sunflowers. Agitation down the nerve, running, fleeing, horror, the death of the child.

America, where have you fallen off the bone, like flesh into cruel use, cruel and immense speculation. Piratical and terrible men, speculation and exploitation, vultures plucking off the sweet flesh. . . . Even the soil of speculation on the earth is the sunlight of a living day, the oils of a living woman. Accumulated phantom in the granary . . . fracture of the heart . . . diminished so we can accept the exact ending . . . you cannot make it lilliputian. A giant is in chains . . . the giant of our people . . . cruel demonic loss of life necessary to certain kinds of cruelty.

"or her either," pointing at me.

The bus driver winked at me. She half ran to the cops and I saw her pointing at me and then the door. They came up to me. "What's this all about?" one of them said.

"Oh, a sick girl on the bus," the driver said. "Just a sick girl got on in El Paso. You should have brought an ambulance maybe. She was pretty sick if you ask me."

"Nobody is asking you," the woman said. "This woman was an accomplice."

"To what?" they said.

"She had a bag."

"Didn't the border cops investigate?"

"She had proper papers," the bus driver said.

"Hurry, she'll get away," the woman said. "She went out that door with her bag."

They turned and went toward the door. I followed them. Had she had time to get out of sight or somewhere? She must have known Denver. She came from there, she kept saying it.

I saw them at the corner looking all ways. The street was sepulchre-ghostly light before the sun, before the diffusion of the sun's light. The buildings were dead white and the street space seemed a ghostly uncertain light in which even the corner of the street shimmered and seemed a straight line. It was a dawn mirage and she was nowhere in sight.

I saw there were many corners she could have turned, jutting out square buildings, an alleyway utterly empty.

It was not a new terror that thus affected me, but the dawn of a more exciting *hope*. This hope arose partly from memory, and partly from present observation.[29]

Now it is a great tree, my body. And the dead rock in cradles in my branches. The tree in Dakota with the dead in it, nurse the dead and the living. Opulent, alive, spreading dark, moving into wounds, cottonwood, entire torn womb of center. Old woman with womb hanging out torn, scarred like an eroded river with the passage, the flood, the badly controlled entrance and flood of children into the mouth of the river.

They stood there looking both ways down the white street. Then they started back and the white woman came out, stalked out the door. "You've let her get away," she said.

"Have you any charges to make against her or her name or anything that she has done?"

"Well, no," she said. "I never saw what was in the bag. Thanks to her accomplice here."

"Did you know her?" they asked me.

"No. I never set eyes upon her before Albuquerque. She was very ill. She was going to a hospital."

"Hospital, my eye," she snorted. "Probably there are her buddies in a dope ring over the border staked out around the corner there if you'd do your duty and look."

"We don't believe there's any crime involved," they said, "unless you have more information . . . or witnesses . . . she must have had documents to pass the border guard. The feds pretty well search everyone suspicious like . . ."

They took off their hats and said goodbye and she turned.

"You're guilty," she said venomously. "You should have turned her in for her own good if for no other reason. I can't figure it out, how you became so close in so short a time. It's something fishy. . . ."

"I don't see anything so terrible in it," I said. "Just a girl in trouble."

"In trouble," she cried. "Is that a . . . what . . . she gave birth in El Paso . . . the terrible smell . . . that's it, and you're responsible for her and for the dead child,

I thrust my arms wildly above and around me in all directions. I felt nothing; yet dreaded to move a step, lest I should be impeded by the walls of a *tomb*.[30]

too. These girls should all be sterilized . . . it's a shame . . . more illegitimate births and abortions . . . what's the country coming to?"

I half ran away from her. Now I felt an anguish . . . where had she gone? How had she disappeared so quickly?

I began walking and as the light grew some stray workers appeared, going to work. I could not ask them if they had seen her. I came to the end of the streets. There were not even any buses or street cars or taxis. They were ghostly empty.

I was frantic now. I didn't know I was weeping.

"Is anything wrong?" an old janitor asked me. "Can I help you?"

"No," I said. "Someone disappeared on the bus."

"Oh, they missed it. They'll be on the next one," he said.

I kept on going down the empty streets until they began to come alive with early Denver workers.

It was too early to go to the sanitarium-prison where my distorted son waited, hardly knowing I would be coming.

But I was going . . . I would carry these witnesses . . . tear open the dismemberment of history . . . expose, cry out . . . I didn't even take the valium.

At nine I got a taxi. The sun came and infused the ghostly streets. I raised my face to it and promised light.

I couldn't leave Denver. I watched all the papers. There was no word of anything happening. Where did she go?

I could not see . . . I was running. I was running to my dead child poisoned by the air, to his corpse to give him true death, my breast of death, milk for the crucified . . . take his poisoned breath, his crippled genes. I was running at last, poisoned I would carry him through atomic death in the skin. Run run come come. It is late, it is early, return the dead child.

The accident is waiting. It is arranged for you to drop dead in an alley. . . . It's on the map of the cops where you are to be run over. It is routine.

Yesterday something broke. There is no skin, you live within a net. What was will be no more . . . eyes see the use and design of everything around him how elegant the junco, everything with its clean elegance, style.

A boat picked me up—exhausted from fatigue—and (now that the danger was removed) speechless from the memory of its horror. Those who drew me on board were my old mates and daily companions—but they knew me no more than they would have known a traveler from the spirit land. My hair, which had been raven black the day before, was as white as you see it now. They say too that the whole expression of my countenance had changed. I told them my story—they did not believe it.[31]

Incomprehensible men! Wrapped up in meditations of a kind which I cannot divine, they pass me by unnoticed. Concealment is utter folly on my part, for the people *will not see.* . . .[32]

Maybe she had friends in Denver. I hoped so at least.

I couldn't get my son out of the institution right away. I had to prepare a place for him, an acceptance of him. My family would never want to look at him every day.

There had been a trial concerning the Nevada tests and some who could prove, without a doubt, that the death of their family was caused by nuclear fallout got what is called recompense. The government knew the danger of fallout, but they lied, they said it was not dangerous to sheep or people . . . to say nothing of the terrible mutations of the genes of the monsters that were born.

Still they want us to be quiet.

I wandered the streets. I looked in the bars on skid row. I thought I would meet her. Around every corner. I even went to the library and the parks . . . it was getting cold.

I didn't dare think of what might happen to her and her sacred bundle. But I heard or saw nothing.

I put the blue knit cap on the bed. I wanted never to lose the bond, the commitment I had felt, moving into a new reality, moving in closer, moving in.

On the fifth day there was a story in the paper about a girl who had come into one of the bars and thrown a dead baby across the bar at the drinking men. She had shouted something and then run out and when they followed they saw only an empty street.

It said the child was not newly born, had been dead a spell. I went to the city desk, the city morgue . . .

Naked she falls from the gutted mines of the Rockies where the trapped dead glow is descending to the long sorrow of hills and plains. She is sitting on the crevasse of prophecy of delphi earth elysian mysteries ceremony of the kernel. New race from rejects and strontium.

Wear him like a banner. Raise his banner up of this beautiful death. He will never have to be worn, to be bone in the field, or skinned alive . . . or broken and smashed and lost, unclaimed. I claim his death.

I shall from time to time continue this journal. It is true that I may not find an opportunity of transmitting it to the world, but I will not fail to make the endeavor. At the last moment I will enclose the MS. in a bottle, and cast it within the sea.[33]

ENDNOTES

1. *The Fall of the House of Usher.*
2. *The Fall of the House of Usher.*
3. *Masque of the Red Death.*
4. *The Pit and the Pendulum.*
5. *The Black Cat.*
6. *The Premature Burial.*
7. *The Pit and the Pendulum.*
8. *The Premature Burial.*
9. *A Tale of the Ragged Mountains.*
10. *A Descent into the Maelstrom.*
11. *The Fall of the House of Usher.*

they were very tight, knew little about it, supposed the child had been buried, never found the mother.

The seventh day there was a story in the paper . . . small as if it was a fantasy . . . could not have happened. A young woman had stood up in the capitol and held a dead baby up to the pure golden dome as if a sacrifice. Had she been arrested? Had she been hospitalized? I called the asylums . . . the city psychiatric offices . . . yes, they had read it in the paper . . . but they had had no details . . . it was thought she had just walked away.

After that, it seemed strange that the front page of the paper had so many pictures of women in El Salvador, Ethiopia, Pakistan, New York, South Dakota, New Mexico—all over the world holding their dead children on their knees, walking long and dread roads . . . living in refugee villages, taking boats out of one violence into another. . . .

She was deep in us all.

The wheat fields and the corn fields burst into bread. Hide and embrace the guerrillas. They are rising in their flesh of necessity, simple hunger. There are no arguments and words now, or debate or confrontation. They are there.

It is a love affair . . . with my country. Always I have lived in her, with her as with a beloved body, mother child husband. Father, lover, child taught me the wonderful earth of the middle country . . . inheritance pirated . . . nakedness always beyond the robber . . . nakedness to nakedness, the conqueror can never be naked. . . . That man who has power never touches your nakedness. We can go to origins that are pure . . . without theft . . . with only gifts, as they gave Cabeza De Vaca. Yes, they meet me as they did him, with the gifts of their naked bodies, robbed of everything but their basic root . . . down to the root. Root hog or die.

12. *The Masque of the Red Death.*
13. *The Tell Tale Heart.*
14. *The Fall of the House of Usher.*
15. *A Descent into the Maelstrom.*
16. *A Descent into the Maelstrom.*
17. *The Facts in the Case of M. Valdemar.*
18. *A Descent into the Maelstrom.*
19. *The Pit and the Pendulum.*
20. *The Pit and the Pendulum.*
21. *The Black Cat.*
22. *The Pit and the Pendulum.*
23. *The Fall of the House of Usher.*
24. *A Tale of the Ragged Mountains.*
25. *A Descent into the Maelstrom.*
26. *The Pit and the Pendulum.*
27. *The Pit and the Pendulum.*
28. *The Fall of the House of Usher.*
29. *A Descent into the Maelstrom.*
30. *The Pit and the Pendulum.*
31. *A Descent into the Maelstrom.*
32. *MS. Found in a Bottle.*
33. *MS. Found in a Bottle.*

AFTERWORD

Meridel Le Sueur, born in 1900, the daughter of radical educator Marian Wharton and stepdaughter of socialist lawyer Arthur Le Sueur, was already a radical in the days of Eugene Debs and John Reed, before World War I. A political activist, a journalist, and a writer of fiction and non-fiction from the late twenties to the fifties, she was blacklisted during the McCarthy period. After sustaining herself through "the dark time" by writing for the left movement magazines and press, such as *Masses and Mainstream* and *The Daily Worker*, she regained a larger audience again in the seventies, thanks partly to the support of the feminist movement and partly to her own political and literary initiatives during the Vietnam era. Her involvement in her writing took on two major aspects: recovering her old works and creating new stories, some of which are only now beginning to see the light of day.

A new generation of editors and friends in the 1970s and early 1980s, including Neala Schleuning, Steve Trimble, Jim Dochniak, Jim Perlman, and myself, along with Elaine Hedges of Feminist Press, labored with Meridel to help restore her early literary works to print, and, in some cases, to put earlier creations into print for the first time. We produced a substantial amount: the volume of poetry *Rites of Ancient Ripening* (first edition, Vanilla Press, 1977); the story collections *Harvest* and *Song for My Time* (first editions, West End Press, 1977); the novel *The Girl* (first edition, West End Press, 1978); the selected writings entitled *Ripening* (first edition, Feminist Press, 1982); the novel *I Hear Men Talking* (first edition, West End Press, 1984); the popular history *North Star Country* (first edition, Deull, Sloan and Pearce, 1945; reprint, University of Nebraska Press, 1984); the family history *Crusaders* (first edition, The Blue Heron Press, 1955; reprint, Minnesota Historical Society, 1984); and several volumes of children's stories first published by Alfred A. Knopf from 1947 to 1954 and republished by Holy Cow! Press from 1985 to 1989.

Meanwhile, Meridel was filling her notebooks with new prose, a radical version of stream-of-consciousness writing. The themes that preoccupied her included the hidden history of the Midwest, the productivity of the land, the role of women as givers of life, and above all an apocalyptic vision of contemporary America. Although she was already contemplating writing a trilogy of novels concerned with these themes, for a period of time at the end of the seventies she concentrated on the present tale, which came to be known as *The Dread Road*. (A portion of the manuscript, in an earlier draft version, was published in the tabloid feminist quarterly *Hurricane Alice*, summer, 1988, 1–3.)

This short novel marked a radical departure from Meridel's earlier work. It treated the Southwest, in which she had first traveled in the early 1960s and to which she had returned in subsequent years. She took the core story from an encounter on a Greyhound bus in the late 1970s with a young woman carrying her dead baby in a little flowered suitcase back to her home for burial. After Meridel had added historical context, a subplot involving the narrator, and other characters and situations, she gave her story a universal background by comparing it to accounts of women and their dead babies she had read in the newspapers or heard elsewhere. Thus the fate of an unknown young woman and her baby would become a miniature epic, to be compared with other tales from around the world.

Like the ancient epics, this story begins in the middle. We don't see the young woman until she has completed almost half her journey from El Paso north to Denver, because the story doesn't yet have a narrator. The narrator, an older woman, gets on the northbound bus in Albuquerque; she is going to visit her son, genetically damaged as a result of nuclear testing in Nevada and instutionalized in Denver. Secondary characters who emerge in the story, such as the social worker and the bus driver, exist partly as foils; they attempt in their own ways to help the young woman but are incapable of understanding her. The journey leads past the site of the Ludlow, Colorado, mine massacre of 1914, in which, we are told, the grandparents of the narrator were killed, and to which the young woman is also obscurely connected. From the rich brew of these intersecting themes of poisoned landscape, genetic damage, and massacre, the young woman and the narrator construct a new vision of a social order, in which the baby's corpse will become a symbol of the regeneration of the oppressed.

The story was intended to be as innovative formally as it is rich in content. Meridel wanted to write not a conventional, linear narrative but one in which different levels of reality could interpenetrate. She sought to do this by conceiving of two secondary texts parallel to the core narrative. One of these would be made up of quotations from the short stories of Edgar Allan Poe, which she took to be prophetic commentaries on the American experience. In the other, "subjective," text, she wanted to include some of the thoughts and feelings of the narrator, who is beset by her own demons as the journey begins. While the two secondary texts—the Poe text and subjective text—would sometimes be wholly distinct from the core text, frequently they would illumine it, providing richer meaning to the work as a whole.

By the early eighties, Meridel had finished the core text. She left the citations from Poe collected but unassembled, and for the subjective text she wrote a substantial portion of a journal, which when it was finally transcribed came to 107 typewritten, single-spaced pages or over five hundred single-paragraph entries.

In the latter stages of the assembly of the manuscript, her daughter, Rachel Tilsen, keyed into a word processor both the core text and the subjective portion, and produced along with Meridel a working version of the core text. Poet-scholar Patricia Clark Smith went over the Poe material, noting the origins of the quotations and suggesting their placement in the text. Rachel, Pat, and I established a working version of the subjective text, using perhaps a third of the original journal material; then Pat, the book's typographer and designer Michael Reed, and I attempted to arrange the subjective text parallel to the core text. Finally Rachel and Meridel reviewed our efforts and offered a number of suggestions as to placement, after which we rearranged the subjective text accordingly.

As I have said, much of the journal material which serves as the basis of the subjective text does not appear in the final version of the book. Some of the material, whether or not we included it in the text, allows us insights into Meridel's thought which are important in themselves. In the rest of this essay I will cite some of the journal passages which touch on Meridel's overall design for the book and her understanding of its relation to the times in which we are living.

Meridel's way of writing is best described as an incitement, a challenge to the reader. She makes this clear in a journal entry which contrasts her dynamic, partisan mode of writing to the traditional linear style which she attributes to the patriarchal establishment.

This is not a story to consume like a steak, digest and excrete. This is a ceremonial, invoked [and] generative, making luminous this murderous space. The linear perspective is flat, objective, seductive, lying. This is the only reality, the agony of the oppressed.

At the same time, she pictures her writing in an organic connection to the reader, like a harvest to be gathered and eaten.

Read this a different way. Story is an apple a squash, a bean tomato. It's a direction at the fork of the road, save you from the dangers, lighten the dangers, get you both and the whole nation and the cosmos through . . . into the fruit. We are going to the fruit.

The composition of the images in the text has a dialectical edge, like much of the rest of Meridel's writing, conditioned as it is by her early training in *reportage*, or political journalism. But here she is talking not about the production of propaganda, but the production of artistic images.

Image of the true American earth . . . rising out of the destruction . . . images of destruction . . . images of rising reality from this. Thesis, antithesis and synthesis.

But above all she admonishes herself to keep things simple.

Don't let it be complicated. It is a bare stark indictment.

Referring to the core story of *The Dread Road*, Meridel has this to say.

The gravid woman coming into milk, the plains, the memory, the corpse. She enters my vision. The growth of this horror in the eye. Her weird and fierce rejection of me, watching me. You're not an agent, she said, or a police woman. No, I said. A conduit, a nerve, a message down my nerves. Down which your angry body goes on a road, a journey, a terrible journey. A smile like an acre of sunflowers. Agitation down the nerve, running, fleeing, horror, the death of the child.

On Meridel's actual meeting with the young woman on the bus, the final version of the story may or may not follow the journal. The "smile like an acre of sunflowers" does not get into the story. We do get essentially the same vignette of the girl's "weird and fierce rejection." The journal also suggests what the author is beginning to make of this whole encounter—"a message down my nerves, down which your angry body goes." The *collaboration* between the girl and the author is already established.

Meridel makes several notes to herself in the course of her journal on how to depict certain scenes. One involves some background on the paternity of the young woman's baby which never gets into the story.

> Make the designs . . . the lover, the memory of the lover from Trinidad to Denver, years before, repeated now. The lover and her mother stinging her to death. The telling of the small tiny reality.

Another concerns the symbolic significance of the young woman as the site of many mythical and real stories.

> She is sitting on the crevasse of prophecy of Delphi earth, Elysian mysteries, ceremony of the kernel. New race from rejects and strontium.

Later, Meridel plots the disappearance of the young woman in Denver as a prelude to her reemergence beyond the ending of the story. She hints at how she will leave things in an air of mystery and anticipation, and *why* she must do things this way.

> Incantation after she leaves [in] Denver, does not find her of course, they have taken her, they have come and taken the child, the great prairie mothers . . . the great mine mothers in the center of turquoise, nothing forgotten for the lost Persephone, returns to bring back spring . . . takes flowers to the underground, the spectres, the sacred ghosts. We must have them. We must ask them to our tables, our beds, our festivals. There is a void without them.

This rich, multi-dimensional effort examines the past, the present and the future. Meridel expresses concerns which go well beyond this single piece of writing in their significance. She begins by discussing her own feelings about America.

> It is a love affair . . . with my country. Always I have lived in her, with her as with a beloved body, mother child husband.

Later, she considers the "conqueror," figured here as the Spanish conquistador.

> Father, lover, child taught me the wonderful earth of the middle country . . . inheritance pirated . . . nakedness always beyond the robber . . . the conqueror can never be naked. . . . That man who has power never touches your nakedness.

She herself has chosen to dwell with the powerless, as did that other traveler, the exceptional Spaniard Cabeza De Vaca, who, shipwrecked with three followers, took a marvelous journey from Louisiana to California and emerged unscathed and full of gifts.

> We can go to origins that are pure . . . without theft . . . with only gifts, as they gave Cabeza De Vaca. Yes, they meet me as they did him, with the gifts of their naked bodies, robbed of everything but their basic root . . . down to the root. Root hog or die.

As Meridel was finishing this journal in 1985, she attended the End of the Decade for Women Conference in Nairobi, Kenya. She used this occasion to comment on the meaning of the story she was finishing, putting it in a modern-day, global context.

> I crouch in the armed hotel in Nairobi curled in death fetus. The great blooming trees, death heads. Make an island of all the skeletons of all the millions of slaves killed. Used, slaughtered like beasts. Now we know where the guns are and what they point at. The rocks of little David in our hands. This is the last turn of the wheel.

Meridel's goal as a writer—it would be easy to compare her with Mother Jones, the legendary labor agitator who appears in the story of Ludlow—is to change things. She rejects the aesthetic view of art as an object, which "makes nothing happen," for a kinetic view of art as a determining subject. Her sense of urgency is arrived at, I think, not merely as a product of years of struggle but as an expression of what that struggle is about.

> I demand that you listen. Be with me on the dread journey, that dread road we must take now. We must all take this journey into each other, into the dark but luminous heart. . . .

—John F. Crawford

A Note on the History of Ludlow

The bus the narrator takes travels parallel to the current route of Interstate 25, north from El Paso, Texas, to Albuquerque and Santa Fe, New Mexico, and on to Trinidad, Pueblo, and Denver, Colorado. Twelve miles north of Trinidad on a rising plain is the turnoff for Ludlow, clearly marked with a sign announcing the Ludlow memorial. The memorial consists of a fenced-in area with a large statue showing a miner, his wife and child, a plaque naming the victims of the Ludlow massacre, and a carved inscription, "In memory of the men, women, and children who lost their lives in freedom's cause at Ludlow, Colorado, April 20, 1914. Erected by the United Mine Workers of America." Alongside the statue is a metal cover on the ground, over the cellar where thirteen miners' wives and their children were found asphixiated at the end of the militia's attack on the miners' campsite that day. It is still possible to lift the metal door and descend the steps into the cellar where the families died.

Back down the highway, in Trinidad in the Greek section of the city cemetery, is the grave of Louis Tikas, with the inscription "Died April 20, 1914, victim of the Ludlow Massacre, organizer for the U.M.W.A., patriot." The graves of other Ludlow victims are situated nearby.

A brief account of the Ludlow strike follows. Around 1910 the United Mine Workers began to concentrate their organizing efforts on the immigrant miners in Colorado, especially in the southeast in Huerfano and Las Animas counties. On September 15, 1913, miners meeting in Trinidad struck for better working conditions, shorter hours, better pay, and company compliance with the state mining laws. They walked out a week later, abandoning their company-owned shacks, and built tent colonies near each of the mining communities. The Ludlow colony, the biggest, housed over one thousand men, women, and children. Clashes developed between company guards and union men until Governor Elias Ammons dispatched the state militia into the region in October. But the militia added to the crisis by joining with the company men, who were importing gun thugs of their own. By mid-April of 1914, most of the militia had been withdrawn again, except for two companies left in Ludlow. One of these was actually made up of coal company men, although it was recognized by the state as a military unit.

On April 20, the two militia companies, armed with high-powered rifles and machine guns mounted on vehicles (including one nicknamed "The Death Special"), attacked the miners, firing down into their camp from Water Tank Hill to the south and moving toward them as the day progressed, keeping up a murderous barrage. Some of the women and children escaped across an arroyo into the Black Hills to the north; others hid in pits dug under the campsite. The tents were set on fire late in the day by advancing company men. Two women and eleven children were asphixiated in a single cellar, while five other strikers and two boys were killed by the troopers during the day's shooting. Among those killed was Louis Tikas, clubbed in the back of the head and subsequently shot three times in the back, according to the inquest held afterwards. It was generally believed he was ordered executed by Lieutenant Karl Linderfelt of the militia.

Partisans of the miners arrived too late to help the devastated colony at Ludlow, but immediately after the massacre they moved into other camps in the region. The militia companies were spread thin and ineffective, hampered by the bad publicity they received after Ludlow. Company property at Forbes, just down the road from Ludlow, was laid waste by a sustained rifle attack and a series of fires. Miners who dug in on the hillsides around the city of Walsenburg to the north held that area from April 27 to April 30, when federal troops belatedly dispatched by President Wilson arrived. A large number of both miners and company officials died before order was finally restored in the two-county region.

Meridel was a teenager when the Ludlow massacre took place. She first heard the story from the workers themselves, when they came to the People's College in Fort Scott, Kansas, later the same year and organized a parade in commemoration of the victims. To this day she remembers her mother, Marian, crying during the parade. Some of Meridel's account in this narrative may actually come from firsthand information; for instance:

> I remember after the massacre there was a terrible passion to get the
> bodies. Don't let the dead children fall into their hands. Don't let
> the mothers, the women, the wives, fall into their murderous hands.
> To get the bodies out of there to Trinidad on that terrible night.

Certainly her view of John D. Rockefeller, bitterly hostile to this day, borrows from memories of the time. Radical reporter John Reed related that the president of Rockefeller's Colorado Fuel and Iron Company received a telegram from Rockefeller after the Ludlow attack which read, "Hearty congratulations on the winning of the strike. I sincerely approve of all your actions."

Of the many accounts of the Ludlow massacre, see John Reed's contemporary article, "Colorado Wars," in *The Education of John Reed* (New York: International Publishers, 1955); Barron Beshoar, *Out of the Depths*, Colorado Labor History Commission (Denver: Denver Labor Federation, 1970); Philip S. Foner, "Revolt of the Miners: Colorado, 1913–1914," in *The AFL in the Progressive Era, 1910–1915*, History of the Labor Movement in the United States, Vol. 5 (New York: International Publishers, 1980); a study of the Greek miners by Zeese Papanikolas, *Buried Unsung* (Salt Lake City: University of Utah Press, 1982); and what may be the last account of Ludlow using oral narrative, Patrick L. Donachy's *A Rendezvous with Shame* (Trinidad: The Inkwell, P.O. Box 966, 1989).

—John F. Crawford

A Note on the Uses of Edgar Allan Poe

By piecing together a patchwork of quotations from Edgar Allan Poe, Meridel calls attention to the enduring Americanness of her own themes and reminds us that certain nightmares lie especially deeply embedded in the American grain.

In the quotations she has chosen, sometimes Meridel evokes a general Poeish quality, for instance by summoning the suggestions of decay, foul things covered up, or unbearable truths brought to light. At other times she clearly wants to call up a specific image with particular ties to the core text— an entombed woman, for example, or a sadist responding to affection with mechanical cruelty; a fool urging us not to dwell on unpleasant thoughts, or the American earth riddled with unquiet graves.

Meridel prepared forty-seven quotations from ten Poe tales, ranging from the most familiar to the little known. In some cases, she indicated where a passage might connect with the core text; in others, we tried to search out such a connection ourselves. For actual inclusion in the final version, we selected thirty-three passages, shortening most of them in the process. Brief notes on each tale and how Meridel used it in her citations follow here.

"The Fall of the House of Usher"—The many connections between this tale and *The Dread Road* begin with the theme of a reluctantly undertaken journey toward a feared place. The narrator's efforts to provide rational explanations for ghostly phenomena and signs of gathering doom at the house of Usher recall the rationalizations of the bus driver and the passengers, especially about the events at Ludlow. Like Usher, like the bereaved young mother, those who appear mad may see most clearly into the heart of things. Also, as is true of a number of the other Poe tales used here, "Usher" deals with the entombment of a living woman, her refusal to shut up and stay dead, and the relentless way Truth has of making itself known.

"The Pit and the Pendulum"—The faceless inquisitors who condemn Poe's poor prisoner and the elaborate machineries of death they devise may recall the absentee owners like Rockefeller and the equipment the coal company detectives brought up to use against the Ludlow miners. Meridel also quotes a passage from this tale affirming the nobility of imaginative people—who may, however, pay dearly for their insights. Significantly, despite the odds, this Poe narrator survives to tell his story of torture.

"A Descent into the Maelstrom"—Another tough narrator who survives, and another tale turning on the idea that what you most fear and seek to avoid is precisely what you must confront. From this story of the fisherman drawn into a giant whirlpool, Meridel chooses quotations that speak not only of inevitability but of how *beautiful* the terrible may be—like the dead baby, like the repressed truth once it is spoken. She also chooses a passage about how survivors may not be believed, no matter how earnestly they try to tell their stories.

"The Tell Tale Heart"—"Murder will out" is again the dominant theme. Meridel also quotes a specific passage where the murderer cannot believe the gendarmes do not hear the thunderous beatings of the victim's heart. (In Poe's tale, of course, they really *don't* hear the pulse, which echoes only in the guilty man's imagination. But Meridel wishes, I think, to evoke the image of the official denial of truths any honest person must acknowledge.)

"The Masque of the Red Death"—This story recounts the futile attempts of aristocrats to escape a plague by barricading themselves inside a castle, where they stage a costume ball; the plague spirit, however, proves to be one of the masquers. Despite the revellers' determination to forget mortality, a chiming clock steadfastly measures the approach of death. Meridel's excerpts evoke the general theme of the inevitable disintegration of a social order founded upon selfishness and denial, but they may also serve to call up more specific images, such as the widely published photograph of John D. Rockefeller dressed in plus-fours, speaking to the press about Ludlow from a lush eastern golf course.

"The Black Cat"—This is another "murder will out" story; it features a female corpse who is not one of Poe's usual neurasthenic heroines but a quite believable middle-class victim of an abusive alcoholic husband. Meridel borrows a passage where the narrator, who progresses from torturing animals to murdering his wife, is musing about the connections between love and violence.

"The Facts in the Case of M. Valdemar" concerns a man who dies while under hypnosis and who, like the ghosts of Ludlow, is able to speak from beyond the grave. His body remains fresh and undecayed until his doctor awakens him from the trance, when the corpse, still speaking, instantly turns into a "mass of putrescence."

From "The Premature Burial" Meridel chooses the phobic narrator's dream, in which he is shown how many people were buried before they were actually dead, and how unquietly these legions lie; she also uses the narrator's terrible awakening from a cataleptic attack to find himself apparently buried alive, the very circumstance he has gone to all lengths to avoid.

"A Tale of the Ragged Mountains" is a story of reincarnation. A man has a waking vision of the massacre in India during which he was slain in a previous life. Meridel quotes the beginning of the vision, where ghostly figures materialize out of the fog, and the explanation of how the hero and his former self are really one soul.

In "MS. Found in a Bottle," the plot parallels that of *The Dread Road* in that the narrator finds himself aboard an eerie ship manned by a ghostly crew, sailing at a furious rate toward some nameless fate which he both fears and eagerly anticipates. The phantom crew refuses to acknowledge his presence; he vows he will keep a journal no matter what befalls him, and tell the world what he discovers. Meridel indicated that this passage should be inserted at the end of the text.

—Patricia Clark Smith

In her journal Meridel refers to Poe in three entries:

> Poe showed us the dread road. I looked, he said, and it seemed they had all drowned. When I got up, looked up, he said, I found everyone had been bound and gagged.

> "Light muffled voice" is the voice of Poe's women after they have been cemented alive in the castle walls. The way her body looked, fortressed, her terrible hips unable to move . . . the sex cemented and hidden.

> Yes, Poe said, my fancy grows charnel in the image of gloom. There is the faint phosphorous image now of decay.

Meridel's view of Poe's writing as a whole may be indebted to the chapter "Edgar Allan Poe" in D. H. Lawrence's *Studies in Classic American Literature* (New York, 1923). One might especially note Lawrence's remark at the beginning of the chapter that Poe's art is concerned with "a disintegrating and sloughing of the old consciousness."

—John F. Crawford

AUTHOR'S NOTE

This is not a book written by one person. This is a communal creation of an image, using the collective experience of a number of people. The collective skill and love which has transformed and illuminated the original chaos of my notes has freed and enriched my whole life's work. This work has freed me of fear, enlarged my courage, and given light to the social images so complex in our birthing world.

The original images were torn out of the subjective pain of the author, telling the story of her true meeting with the woman on a bus who carried a dead child she had just birthed in the rest room of the bus station. Opposite this was the subjective agony of the woman telling the terrible experience, reflecting the time, and along with this, quotations from Edgar Allan Poe in which he reflected the dread road of his time and the continuing, hidden buried death in America.

Through the coming together of the collective, in its entire imagination and skill, everyone has made an essential contribution, mingling in the creation of the whole. The various skills of the four gestators of the Dread Road, Rachel Tilsen, John Crawford, Pat Smith, and Michael Reed, have illumined this image. Rachel Tilsen has hewed out the images from the chaotic notes. John Crawford, with his genius not only as editor, but as collaborator, has joined in fiercely diving deep and bringing up and giving shape to the many illuminations of the tortured images of the birthing, the converging of the chaos of the writer.

This great litany of collective work includes the woman who persisted in giving her image of the dead child she carried from the poisoned fields, her lifting of the image out of the personal and private grief, and it also images a reader who is not only private but cries out collectively and lifts the image to the communal consciousness of all the people.

The form and intuition of the future is in the relationship, the collective building, of a social image—impossible for the isolated, competitive, alienated consciousness of cultural imperialism. The creations of the future will be songs of the collective experience. I don't know how to describe their creators except as editors, illuminators, synthesizers. This is done now in music and dance.

I believe this is the way that the ancient sagas were written, lifted from the personal to the tribal, a communal reflection of a collective image. . . . Goethe said it took a hundred years for the people's folk image to enter his work. Lorca said that the writer, the tribal poet, should take the collective image of the people, give it form and return it to the people. Upton Sinclair sent Ella Reeve Bloor into the stockyards to reflect, bringing back in her working class woman's sensibility the images of the horrors of the slaughterhouse which he as an isolated writer would not reflect, and the great emotional power of *The Jungle* displays this communal wealth of mutual skills. John Steinbeck used the chaotic notes of the woman lettuce workers, whose genius he never dislocated, in writing *Grapes of Wrath*.

This probing and creative conjunction of the images of our social agony, of birth, of becoming a new world, this collective global consciousness, is the lighting and movement of our time, the collective converging toward the birth of a new humanity.

—Meridel Le Sueur

CONTRIBUTOR'S NOTE

In the 1970s Meridel told me about a bus ride she had taken from Albuquerque to Denver. There was a young woman on the bus carrying a dead baby in a little flowered suitcase. I began to notice stories in the paper about young women with their dead babies, carrying and burying their dead children. This story has become universal to me.

My grandmother and my mother started telling me the story of Ludlow, Colorado, when I was a little girl. I always understood that surviving miners went all over the country to tell the story. It wasn't in many newspapers and what accounts there were often described the miners as "troublemakers" or "violent protestors" or "criminals." I was told they were working 12 to 16 hours a day, seven days a week, and their attempt to form a union and improve their working conditions was their crime.

Meridel has welded the violence of the past into the violence of the present. I must tell the stories of those who have died apparently unknown and unremembered. I must remember them all.

—Rachel Tilsen

MERIDEL LE SUEUR was born in Murray, Iowa, in 1900. The daughter of radical educator Marian Wharton and stepdaughter of radical lawyer Arthur Le Sueur, she divided her childhood between a socialist community at People's College in Fort Scott, Kansas, and St. Paul, Minnesota. As a teenage girl she lived briefly in Emma Goldman's commune in Greenwich Village, then worked as a movie double in Hollywood and an actor and director in grassroots theater elsewhere in California. She began publishing her stories at the end of the 1920s, and through the next decade wrote for a variety of magazines, from left wing (*New Masses*, *Anvil*, *Partisan Review*) to mainstream (*The Dial*, *Scribner's Magazine*, *American Mercury*). She published a story collection, *Salute to Spring*, in 1940; a popular history of the Midwest, *North Star Country*, in 1945; and five volumes of children's stories for Alfred A. Knopf from 1947 to 1954.

Her name was appearing on political blacklists by this time; soon she was categorically denied access to mainstream publication. While she continued to write for left magazines, several of her books were also published by political supporters: *Crusaders*, a chronicle of the lives of her parents, in 1955; and *Corn Village*, a selection of her best stories, in 1970. After 1977, a new generation of publishers worked with her to produce a poetry collection, *Rites of Ancient Ripening* (1977); two novels, *The Girl* (1978) and *I Hear Men Talking* (1984); and two story collections, *Harvest* and *Song for My Time* (published as two volumes, 1977; combined into one volume, 1982) and *Ripening* (1982). The earlier volumes *Salute to Spring*, *North Star Country*, and *Crusaders* were reissued during the same period.

In 1990, West End Press issued new editions of the novel *The Girl* and the story collection *Harvest and Song for My Time* (expanded to twice the original size and retitled *Harvest Song*). *Harvest Song* won an American Book Award from the Before Columbus Foundation in 1991.

After living many years in St. Paul, Meridel Le Sueur now resides with her family in Hudson, Wisconsin, just across the Minnesota state line.